W9-ASM-473

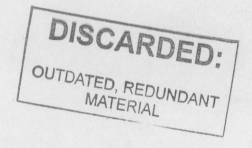

PALM BEACH COUNTY
LIBRARY SYSTEM
3650 Summit Boulevard
West Palm Beach. FL 33406-4198

Lucky Dog

Twelve Tales of Rescued Dogs

Lucky Dog

Twelve Tales of Rescued Dogs

Scholastic Press / New York

For each copy of this book sold, all royalty amounts (estimated range of $0.22–$1.60 depending on edition) are being donated to RedRover, an animal welfare nonprofit, whose mission is to bring animals out of crisis and strengthen the bond between people and animals through emergency sheltering, disaster relief services, financial assistance, and education. Learn more: RedRover.org

No part of this publication may be reproduced, stored in a retrieval system, or transmitted in any form or by any means, electronic, mechanical, photocopying, recording, or otherwise, without written permission of the publisher. For information regarding permission, write to Scholastic Inc., Attention: Permissions Department, 557 Broadway, New York, NY 10012.

Library of Congress Cataloging-in-Publication Data

Lucky dog : twelve tales of rescued dogs / [by Kirby Larson . . . et al.]
   p. cm.
  Summary: A collection of stories about the Pawley Rescue Center, where rescued dogs find their way into hearts and homes.
  ISBN 978-0-545-55451-0
  1. Dog rescue — Juvenile fiction. 2. Dog adoption — Juvenile fiction. 3. Dogs — Juvenile fiction. [1. Dog rescue — Fiction. 2. Dog adoption — Fiction. 3. Dogs — Fiction.] I. Larson, Kirby.
  PZ5.L973 2013
  813.008 — dc23

                                   2013011309

"Like an Old Sweater" © 2014 by Kirby Larson
"The Incredibly Important True Story of Me!" © 2014 by Tui T. Sutherland
"Who Wants a Dog?" © 2014 by Ellen Miles
"Bird Dog and Jack" © 2014 by Leslie Margolis
"Buddy's Forever Home" © 2014 by Teddy Slater
"Lab Partner: An Adoption in Six Scenes" © 2014 by Michael Northrop
"Chihuahua Rescue!" © 2014 by Randi Barrow
"Foster's Home" © 2014 by Jane B. Mason & Sarah Hines Stephens
"Big Dogs" © 2014 by C. Alexander London
"Package Deal" © 2014 by Marlane Kennedy
"The Heart Dog" © 2014 by Elizabeth Cody Kimmel
"Farfel" © 2014 by Allan Woodrow

All rights reserved. Published by Scholastic Press, an imprint of Scholastic Inc., *Publishers since 1920.* SCHOLASTIC, SCHOLASTIC PRESS, and associated logos are trademarks and/or registered trademarks of Scholastic Inc.

12 11 10 9 8 7 6 5 4 3 2   13 14 15 16 17 18 19/0

Printed in the U.S.A.   23
First printing, February 2014
Designed by Jeannine Riske

Table of Contents

Like an Old Sweater
by Kirby Larson

Troy couldn't believe it. He'd only just arrived and now his aunt wanted to send him off with her two neighbor kids, Sophia and Milo.

"I should finish unpacking," he said. Not that he had that much to unpack. All their moves had taught Dad and him to travel light.

Dad. Troy glanced at the clock in Tottie's kitchen. He would be in the air still, on his way to Germany for his latest deployment. This time, Troy couldn't go along. He had to do the whole "new kid in town, new kid in school" thing all by himself. At least school didn't start for another week.

"The best way to get settled in is to get involved." Tottie shooed him outside. "Have fun!" She closed the front door before Troy could say anything else.

"It's nice of you to volunteer," Sophia said. "We can always use extra help at the rescue center."

There wasn't anything voluntary about it. Tottie had practically shoved Troy out the door. It wasn't like she was mean. After all, she'd given up her home office so Troy could have a bedroom. But he could tell that the last thing she wanted was to keep her eleven-year-old nephew while her brother was deployed for eighteen months. Why else would she have tried to get rid of him when he'd just arrived? Troy felt like one of those ugly sweaters his grandma used to knit for him and Dad. Like something for the giveaway box.

Sophia and Milo chattered away at him the entire walk to the Pawley Rescue Center. Inside, Sophia introduced Troy to their dad, Mr. Cole. "He started the Center," she said proudly.

"Glad to meet you, Troy," said Mr. Cole. "What are you kids planning today? We got a big donation of dog crates that need scrubbing."

"Not again!" Milo groaned. "We did that last weekend."

"Yeah," added Sophia. "And we still have dishpan hands!"

Mr. Cole laughed. "Okay. Okay. How about some dog playtime?"

"Come on!" Milo tugged on Troy's sleeve and led him through some kind of workroom, filled with the dog crates Mr. Cole had mentioned, out a set of double doors to a big, fenced-in grassy area.

Sophia unlatched the gate and she and Milo went right in. A black Lab ran up to them, chomping on a slobbery tennis ball. "Drop, Barkly," said Milo. The dog obeyed. Milo picked up the slobbery ball and, without even wiping his hands on his jeans, threw it for him. Gross.

Sophia grabbed a rope toy and whistled for a pony-sized dog. "How are you today, Moose?" She played tug-of-war with Moose while Milo threw the ball over and over for Barkly.

Troy hung around by the gate as some other volunteers arrived and began playing with the dogs, too. No one seemed to notice him standing there. He felt more and more like one of those unwanted sweaters.

He found his way back to the room with the crates. The other volunteers were probably as excited about scrubbing them out as Sophia and Milo had been. But Troy didn't mind this kind of work. And he better get used to working alone. He found a pair of rubber gloves and some cleaner.

He began to fill a bucket with water. Then he thought he heard something. He turned off the faucet to listen. It was knocking. Like someone was rapping at that door over there. Troy hesitated. Should he open it? Maybe one of the volunteers had gotten locked out.

Troy peeled off the rubber gloves and pushed the door open. No one was there.

He stuck his head out and looked around. "Hello?" he called. "Did you want in?" No one answered. He shrugged and began to close the door.

Then he noticed a crate. Probably another donation. Troy stepped out and picked it up by the handle on top.

It whined.

"What?" He bobbled the crate, nearly dropping it. He peeked in through the wire mesh on the side. Two sad brown eyes peered back. "I guess I better bring you inside," Troy said.

When he set the crate down, he saw a letter taped to it. Troy peeled it off and opened it. "This is Oscar," the letter began. "He's been my best friend for six years. But I'm getting old. And where I'm going doesn't allow dogs. I know you will find him a good home."

Troy scanned the letter again. It wasn't signed. He peeked into the crate. "Oscar?" he said.

The dog stayed put but those sad brown eyes followed Troy's every move. Troy pressed his fingers against the mesh. Oscar snuffled at them with his cold wet nose.

"It's okay," Troy said, even though he knew it wasn't okay for poor Oscar. How could it be? Separated from his friend. Having to go to a new place. "It *will* be okay," he promised Oscar. "They're crazy about dogs here."

Oscar made a little chuffing sound.

"Do you want out?" Troy asked. What were the rules about getting dogs out of crates? He had no idea. But he knew someone who would.

"Wait here," Troy said. "I'll be back." He ran back to the play area. Sophia was picking up a handful of yellow tennis balls. Troy tapped her on the arm. "Um, can you come with me?" he asked.

"In a sec." She stuffed the balls in a mesh sack and hung it on a peg. "Someone brought in some pug puppies and I want to go see them."

"It's important." He tugged on Sophia's arm.

"More important than puppies?" she asked.

"Just come," he said. Finally she followed him into the back room.

"Who's this?" She knelt down and peered into the crate. "Poor baby," she cooed, unlatching the crate door. "Come on out."

The dog did not come out.

"His name is Oscar." Troy was pretty sure Oscar didn't like being called a baby. He showed her the letter.

"He's a Cavalier King Charles spaniel," Sophia said. "Very loyal to their people." Sophia patted her knees to get Oscar to come to her. "His little heart is probably broken." She kept patting her knees but Oscar stayed in the crate.

Troy peered over Sophia's shoulder. "That doesn't seem to be working."

"Let's try a treat." Sophia hopped up, ran to a cupboard, and pulled out a handful of doggy cookies. "Want one of these, buddy?"

Oscar didn't move.

"Wow." Sophia rocked back on her heels. "He's really upset. I better go find Dad." She hopped up and hurried away.

Troy ducked his head to look inside the crate. Oscar was kind of small but his ears nearly touched the ground. He was a patchwork of black and white and brown fur. "Hey, Oscar," Troy said softly. "Why don't you come out?"

Oscar shivered but stayed where he was.

Troy eased onto his stomach in front of the crate's door. Now Troy could see the reddish-brown eyebrows that topped Oscar's dark eyes. "It's no fun leaving your home, is it?" Troy rested his chin on the tile floor. "Believe me, I know." Troy thought about Dad and something damp and cold leaked out of his eyes. Oscar scooted forward. He licked Troy's face. Troy patted the dog's fur. It was so soft. Like that angora yarn Grandma used to knit with.

"Wanna come the rest of the way out?" Troy said. He inched away from the crate. Oscar kept following, kept licking. When the tip of his feathery tail was out, Troy sat up, cross-legged. Oscar stepped over Troy's legs and curled up in his lap. He rubbed his muzzle against Troy's jeans a few times, then settled with a loud sigh. Troy scratched behind Oscar's floppy ears.

Sophia came rushing back, her dad in tow. "You got him out of the crate!" she exclaimed. "That's amazing."

Mr. Cole knelt down, rubbing Oscar's ears, too. "Hey there, buddy," he said. His tone was calm and warm. Oscar's tail waggled a little. But he stayed close to Troy. "Looks like you've made a friend," Mr. Cole said.

Troy stayed very still so he wouldn't scare Oscar away. "He's even got one freckle on his nose," he said. "Like me."

Mr. Cole nodded. "That's called the queen's thumbprint," he said. "This breed was a favorite of English royalty."

"He came with a letter." Sophia showed it to her father.

Mr. Cole sighed. "I wish more retirement homes would take dogs. It would save a lot of heartaches. For people and dogs alike."

Oscar wiggled around in Troy's lap. "I think he's nervous," Troy said. "I mean, about all the new faces."

"I think you're right." Sophia backed away. "Maybe you're part dog whisperer!"

Mr. Cole ran his hands through his wiry hair. "Dr. Mehta's gone home for the day. We'll have to leave Oscar here tonight. She can check him out in the morning." He patted Troy on the back. "Do you want to take him over to the overnight boarding area?"

Troy held on to Oscar and stood up, careful not to drop him. He followed Mr. Cole. Oscar seemed okay to go back into another crate, but when Troy stepped away, he whimpered.

Troy looked into the crate. He recognized that look in Oscar's eyes. He didn't say anything but he promised himself to come back as soon as he could in the morning. So Oscar wouldn't have time to get too lonely.

Troy, Sophia, and Milo helped Mr. Cole close up for the night. Then the Coles drove Troy home. Tottie ordered in pizza but Troy could only eat one piece. The olives reminded him of Oscar's dark eyes.

Troy finished unpacking after dinner, putting things in the same drawers he did at home. He put Dad's picture — the one of him in his fatigues — on top of the dresser, like always, and hung his Ichiro poster on the wall opposite his bed, where he could see it first thing every morning.

At home, Troy fell asleep to the sound of that old Douglas fir brushing against his window, and the furnace sighing as it shut off for the night. Tottie's house was so new and quiet, he could hear her keyboard click-click-clicking even through the bedroom walls. It was hard to sleep.

Troy thought about Oscar. It must be hard for him to sleep too, in a strange place. At least Troy knew he had a home with Tottie while Dad was away. Poor Oscar didn't know where his home would be.

The next morning, Troy gobbled up some pancakes. "Would it be okay if I went over to the rescue center?" he asked. "I mean, I didn't finish scrubbing out those crates yesterday."

Tottie's right eyebrow arched up. "Well, sure." She poured herself another cup of coffee. "But they have other volunteers, you know."

Troy took his plate to the sink. "I know," he said, rinsing it off. "But I feel like I should finish what I started."

"You got that from your dad. Not from me." Tottie chuckled. "Be home by four?" she suggested.

Troy nodded. "Four."

He brushed his teeth quickly and was jogging into the Center's parking lot about fifteen minutes later. Sophia answered his knock.

"He's doing great," she said.

"Who?" Troy asked.

She nudged him. "Oscar, of course."

"Okay." Troy shrugged. "I'm just here to finish cleaning crates."

Sophia looked at him. "You want to help me today?" she asked.

"Doing what?"

She pointed toward the dog run. "Playing with all those guys, you big goof."

Troy wiped his hands on his jeans. "Is there another option?"

"Sure. You can go help get Oscar ready to go."

"Go?" The pancakes in Troy's stomach turned to cement. "Go where?"

"His new home." Sophia clapped her hands. "He got adopted. Already! Isn't that great?"

"Great." Troy chewed on his lip. "Uh. Where's he going?"

"I don't know." Sophia grabbed a bag of balls. "That's Dad's department."

Troy followed her to the play area. There was Oscar, flat on his tummy, his muzzle resting on his front paws. Alone, in the corner. His sad brown eyes followed Troy every step of the way. His feathery tail wagged when Troy plopped down in front of him.

"So, you've got a new home already." Troy leaned in, lifting up one of those heavy ears. "I hope it's forever," he whispered. "And that you never have to leave your family. Ever again."

Oscar turned his head to lick Troy's cheek. Then he cocked his head and looked straight at Troy, as if he understood what Troy was saying.

So, Troy began to tell him. Everything. About all the big spaces in his heart. About missing Dad. About feeling like the odd sock out at Tottie's. About wondering if he'd make any friends at his new school. "And Sophia doesn't count," he whispered. "She has to be nice to me. We're neighbors."

Oscar crawled onto his lap, nestling his head on Troy's arm.

"But we're lucky, right?" Troy said. "I've got Tottie, and you've got your —" He cleared his throat. "Your new family."

Troy ruffled the soft fur on top of Oscar's head. "Maybe I can dog-sit you if your new family goes on vacation or something."

Troy started to ease Oscar out of his lap but the dog pushed himself tighter against him. Some dogs dug holes in gardens; Oscar had dug a hole in Troy's heart. He should be happy that Oscar had a new family. He took one last sniff of Oscar's fur. It was a good smell. Like the smell of home.

Sophia and Milo came over to him.

"Is his family here?" Troy asked, proud that his voice was strong.

Sophia nodded. "Can you bring him to the reception room?" she asked.

Troy blinked. "Maybe you should take him," he said. "I'm new here."

"I think he'd rather you carried him," Sophia said. "Come on."

Troy stood up, carefully holding Oscar, and followed Sophia. Milo walked next to him.

"It's a good family," Milo said. Troy nodded, knowing Milo wanted to make him feel better.

They passed through the doors to the reception room.

"Tottie?" What was she doing here? "I said I'd be home by four." Troy shifted Oscar in his arms.

She tugged on her baseball cap. "Well, I thought you'd need some help getting home."

"Help?" Troy was confused. "I know the way."

"But look at all the stuff you'd have to carry."
She pointed to a stack of dog supplies on the
counter.

Troy stared at her.

Then Sophia burst out laughing. "You're Oscar's
new family, you ninny." She ruffled the fur on
Oscar's head.

"Oscar's mine?" He couldn't believe it. Yesterday
morning, he didn't even like dogs, and now he
was going to be owned by one. He glanced over at
Tottie. "I mean, ours."

"Well, I'm hoping you'll let me take him for
a walk now and again." Tottie smiled. "But it's
pretty clear that Oscar is all yours."

"I should ask Dad," Troy said.

Tottie wrapped her arm around his shoulder. "I
called him this morning. He gave the whole thing
one big thumbs-up."

Oscar licked Troy's face. Troy looked at his
aunt. At his new friends. Their smiles warmed
him up like a wool sweater.

And not the kind that Grandma made.

🐾 🐾 🐾

Kirby Larson shares her home in Washington with Winston the Wonder Dog, a Cavalier King Charles spaniel. Kirby has won many awards for her books, including a Newbery Honor for *Hattie Big Sky*. Winston is peeved that her latest book, *Duke*, is about a German shepherd and not about him.

The Incredibly Important True Story of Me!

by Tui T. Sutherland

I knew there was going to be trouble the minute I saw him, which was the minute that tall man carried me over to the kennel and said, "I bet you two will get along." Immediately I said at the top of my lungs, "WHAT? WHAT? DO YOU SEE THE SIZE OF THAT DOG? DO YOU SEE THE SIZE OF ME? How can you expect me to share space with a HIPPOPOTAMUS DISGUISED AS A CANINE? All that fur isn't fooling ME. I am going to get SQUASHED BY GIANT PAWS and THEN where will the world be? ME-LESS, I tell you! I DEMAND A PRIVATE KENNEL! DON'T YOU KNOW WHO I AM?"

But he just patted me on the head and said, "Yes, yes, we hear you, cutie," which is so human. They're always hearing but not listening, as if one bark is the same as another. I have VERY IMPORTANT things to say! As a matter of fact, EVERYTHING I have to say is very important! But I might as well woof it all at the moon, I tell you.

So he sticks me in this kennel with this GREAT BIG GALUMPHER who has to be the biggest dog I've ever seen, all shaggy gray-and-white fur so I can't even see his eyes. And I'm no puppy born yesterday. I'm a whole ten months old. I know you can't trust anyone whose eyes you can't see. Anything could be going on under that mop! Is he looking at me? Or worse, is he NOT LOOKING AT ME?

I gave him my Extra-Fierce Face. It is the Face I used to strike terror into the hearts of those two cats I lived with before our owner, the Frightfully Old Lady What Smelled Like Sneezing and Oranges, took them off with her to live someplace warm where she said I couldn't go because of all my woofing.

So it was the Pawley Rescue Center for me, but I wasn't worried, because have you seen my adorable face? Have you seen my splendid ears? Have you seen my glorious puff of golden fur? I am Pomeranian Perfection Personified and I knew someone would want to take me home before you could say CUTEST DOG EVER WOOF.

That is, I wasn't worried until I saw the woolly mammoth I had to share a kennel with.

He didn't look very alarmed by my Extra-Fierce Face, I must say.

But it was hard to tell under all that fur. I think he was just staring at me, but he could also have been asleep sitting up.

"This is how it is!" I barked at him. "I'm taking this half of the kennel!" I strutted from one wall to the other, making sure the food and water bowls were in my half. If I were a boy dog, I'd have peed all over the place to let him know it was all mine, but I am a girl dog and much more genteel and refined and sensible than that.

"You stay over there!" I woofed. "Got it?"

And then he stood up. Holy paws! He was even bigger than I thought!

"I'M ABOUT TO BE EATEN ALIVE!" I hollered, flinging myself at the kennel door.

"Hey," the giant said softly. "I'm Bear."

"I'M ABOUT TO BE EATEN ALIVE BY A BEAR!" I yelled.

"Actually, I'm an Old English sheepdog," he said.

Apparently no one was rushing to my rescue, so I sat down and gave him my Stern Face. "You are excessively big," I informed him. "And hairy."

"I know," he said. "Although you're pretty furry, too."

"My fur is essential to my adorableness," I explained. "Yours is extremely suspicious."

He nodded thoughtfully. "It is a problem," he said. "My last people were allergic to it. That's why I'm here. Waiting for a home. But nobody wants big dogs." He lowered his vast black nose toward me and sniffed. "You smell nice. Like outside and sunshine. What's your name?"

"Foxtrot," I said. "It's a dance. Because the Old Lady thought I was going to be ever so very elegant and poised, ha-ha, rrrruff."

Bear lay down. "Tell me everything about yourself, Foxtrot." His floppy gray ears twitched forward. Even though I couldn't see his eyes, and even though I'd never seen one before, I was pretty sure this was a Listening Face.

That is when I decided that Bear was my One and Only Truest Best Friend in the World and we would never be parted NEVER NEVER NEVER not even for a MILLION LIVER TREATS so JUST TRY IT, people. FIERCE FACE.

Nine days later, the Family of Doom showed up.

Oh, they didn't look like a Family of Doom. They looked like an ordinary mom-dad-brother-sister, but I should have sniffed them out all the same.

"Look!" squealed the little one with pigtails. "Aw! They're all cute and snuggled together!"

I was sitting between Bear's front paws at the time, because all that fur made them marvelous pillows, plus he was warm and his breath smelled like meat YUM. But I was in the middle of a story and had no intention of being interrupted.

"So THEN," I said, "THEN the black cat was like, I bet you can't pull that white cloth off that table, and I was all, yes I can! Of course I can! And she was like, purrrrrrreally, let me see, and I was like, just watch me! And I grabbed it in my teeth! And I RRRRed it and RRRRRFFed and SCRRRRRFFed it and tugged and tugged with all my might!"

"Uh-oh," said Bear.

"Uh-oh is right," I said. "The white cloth flew off the table! Because I am very strong! But so did the lamp. And the picture frames. And a basket of very smelly dead flowers. There was crashing! And smashing! And mess! In all directions! And when I got out from under the cloth, the black cat was looking ever so smug and the Old Lady had appeared wearing the Maddest Face You've Ever Seen. And then I had to stay in the yard for hours and not one person cared no matter how much I howled."

"Poor Foxtrot," Bear said sympathetically.

"Indeed," I said. "Poor ME. So that was day six. On the *seventh* day —"

But then the kennel door squeaked open and the two little people came in with the tall shelter man.

The littler one crouched down and said, "Hi, puppy!" and held out her hand. "I'm Willamina, and this is my brother, Wyatt." The bigger one blinked at me through his glasses.

I've never met a hand I didn't want to sniff, so I popped out of Bear's paws and went over to investigate.

"Smells like lollipops," I reported to Bear. I licked Willamina's thumb. "And crayons. And glitter glue. And pancakes."

"I had pancakes once," Bear said mournfully. "My family kept putting food on the counter and then getting mad when I ate it." He sighed. "It was very confusing."

"That over there is Bear," I informed Willamina, who had something like a Listening Face on but you can't really expect too much from humans. "He is my One and Only Truest Best Friend in the World."

Wyatt crouched down and held out his hand, too.

"What does he smell like?" Bear asked.

"Books," I said. "And pears. Also pancakes. And a piano. The Old Lady had a piano, which, it turned out, was Not For Climbing On Get Off You Ridiculous Dog! Now there's a story I haven't —"

"I love her!" Willamina cried.

And before I knew it — before I could tell Bear about my adventures with the piano, before I could tell him he could have *my* pancakes if I ever had any and *I* wouldn't get mad, before I could even say good-bye — suddenly I was up in the air and sailing off down the hallway in the tall man's arms.

"BEAR!" I yowled. "BEAR! THEY ARE ABSCONDING WITH ME! IT'S A POMERANIAN-NAPPING! DO SOMETHING!"

"Foxtrot!" he called sadly. "I'll miss you!"

"THIS SHALL NOT STAND!" I hollered. "BEAR! I'LL COME BACK FOR YOU! I'LL DIG A TUNNEL! I'LL LEARN TO FLY! I'LL ESCAPE AND SET YOU FREE AND WE'LL RUN AWAY, BEEEEEEEEE-AAAAAAAAARRRRR —"

And then the door swung closed and it was official: I belonged to the Family of Doom.

WELL. You better believe I had something to say about that.

"Take me back!" I ordered the mom, who was driving the car. "My best friend is back there! I haven't even told him about the first time I saw snow or the squirrel conspiracy or throwing up in the Old Lady's car!"

"Noisy little thing, isn't she?" said the dad in what I would definitely call a Concerned Voice.

"Don't worry, puppy," Willamina said, patting the top of the crate. "You'll like our house."

"I WILL NOT BE BRIBED!" I yapped.

And then we got to their house and I had to admit that for a bribe, it was a pretty good effort, because the yard was something like a MILLION times bigger than the Old Lady's garden with all the Stop Digging Up My Dahlias You Pernicious Fur-ball flowers, plus it was all grass and space for running and smells of squirrels and three whole trees and tennis balls hiding in the bushes and —

"No! You cannot replace my One and Only Truest Best Friend with a backyard, no matter how splendid!" I barked. And I sat down on their back porch and complained and barked and yowled until Wyatt took me inside to the food and water bowls. I deigned to hush up long enough to eat some kibble, but only to lull them into a false sense of security, was my plan.

While they all made dinner, I investigated the whole house. Every few minutes I bolted back to the kitchen barking, "I WILL NOT BE IGNORED!" at the top of my lungs. This was fantastically effective in that they jumped every single time, which was hilarious, and also once the mom dropped a whole bowl of shredded cheese and I got to help clean it up lickety-split YUM.

After the fifth time, I lurked in the next room to spy on them.

"Maybe this wasn't such a good idea," said the dad, rubbing his forehead.

"Give her a few days to settle down," said the mom.

"I SHALL NEVER GIVE IN!" I yowled, sprinting off to check the exits one more time.

After dinner — during which only HALF of ONE meatball was smuggled under the table — Willamina took me up to her room.

"This bed is for you," she said, pointing to a dark green snuggly dog bed, which was just the perfect color for my fur.

"Hrrmph," I said, sniffing it. Willamina's own bed was covered in glitter stickers and a green comforter with white stars. I jumped up on her pillow and gave her a very reasonable speech about tearing apart best friends and how no one had ever listened to me like Bear and it wasn't fair and all of that.

"Foxtrot!" Willamina cried. "Calm down!"

"Maybe she's nervous about being in a new place," Wyatt suggested from the doorway.

"NERVOUS!" I yapped. "I'm never nervous! I am fierce! I am intrepid! I will bark like this until you take me back to Bear!"

But later that night I discovered it is hard to be intrepid and fierce in the dark in a strange dog bed in a strange house with no big shaggy paws to curl around you and no listening ears to tell about your dreams. I put my paws over my nose and wondered where the tragic whimpering noises were coming from.

"Poor Foxtrot," Willamina whispered from above me. "Don't be sad. We're really nice, I promise."

Oh. The noises were coming from me.

27

The door creaked open and Wyatt snuck inside. "It's okay, little dog," he whispered, crouching to pat my head.

Willamina's hands lifted me into her bed. She stroked my ears and scratched my tummy.

"She sounds lonely," Wyatt said. He sat on the floor and gave me his hand to gnaw on.

"I think she misses that sweet big shaggy dog," Willamina said.

My heart skipped a beat. I licked her nose as vigorously as I could. She understood me! As well as a human could anyway. It was an absolute miracle.

"I'll ask if we can go visit him tomorrow," Wyatt whispered.

Maybe it is possible to have three *One and Only Truest Best Friends in the World,* I thought. I wrapped my paws around Wyatt's hand and fell asleep in Willamina's arms.

"She's always much calmer when she's with Bear," said the tall shelter man, watching us.

"Oh, really?" said the dad, but to be fair, we were in the Throes of Our Great Joyous Reunion, so naturally there was leaping and cavorting and yipping and spinning and bouncing, and also what Bear was doing, which was standing still looking at me with the biggest grin on his shaggy lovable face, oh I could SNUG HIM FOREVER.

"Some dogs just click with each other," said the mom, leaning on the fence around the shelter yard.

"I knew she missed him," Willamina said. She picked up one of the balls and threw it, and Bear obligingly bounded after it.

"I'm sure she'll settle down after being with you for a few days," said the shelter man. "Or, of course, you could always take Bear home with you, too." He smiled as if this was a joke, AS IF IT WASN'T LITERALLY THE GREATEST IDEA OF ALL TIME.

"Absolutely not," said the dad, but it was too late. I'd seen the mom and Willamina and Wyatt all light up. If they'd had tails, they'd have been wagging hopefully. I wagged my own little tail as fast as I could and barked, "I'll be good! I promise! Well, I'll try! Bear will help me! He's good at being good! Much better than I am!"

After that there was a lot of human talking but guess who won? The Forces of Good and Friendship and Loyalty, that's who!

"I'm pretty sure this is not a good idea," said the dad as we all piled into the car. All of us! ALL OF US!

"I'm pretty sure it's wonderful," said the mom, burying her hands in Bear's fur and smooching the top of his head.

"Me too!" chorused Wyatt and Willamina.

"Me too me too me too!" I yipped, jumping up to lick all their faces. "Bear, wait till you see their backyard! Bear, their kibble tastes like bacon! Bear, maybe you'll get to sleep on Wyatt's bed! Because there isn't any room on Willamina's bed because that's where I'll be sleeping is what I've decided. BEAR, GUESS WHAT?!"

Bear squashed his shagginess into the backseat and beamed at me. "What?"

"It turns out," I said, "that humans can have Listening Faces, too." I licked Willamina's hand and off we went home, me and my three Truest Best Friends in the World.

Tui T. Sutherland is the author of several books for young readers, including the dragon series Wings of Fire, the Menagerie trilogy, the Pet Trouble series about mischievous dogs, and three books in the bestselling Seekers series (as part of the Erin Hunter team). In 2009, she was a two-day champion on *Jeopardy!* She lives in Massachusetts with her wonderful husband, two adorable sons, and one very patient dog, who has the most excellent Listening Face. To learn more about Tui's books, visit her online at www.tuibooks.com.

Who Wants a Dog?
by Ellen Miles

I never even wanted a dog.

Some people get gooey-eyed over those pictures of puppies sitting in wheelbarrows or peeking out from behind flowerpots. My sister, Hannah, did. I, Heather, did not.

Yes, we're twins. But we're not anywhere near identical. She's smaller, with straight dark hair. My hair is blond and curly. I'm a good writer; she's good at math. And as much as she loves animals, I love going fast, whether I'm on skis, a bike, or even just my own two feet. I hold the 500-yard-dash record for our entire school, and even though my bike is old and clunky, I'm already in training for my dream: to be the first woman to win the

Tour de France. All in all, the only things Hannah and I have in common are a shared room, a habit of chewing our fingernails, and a way of sensing how the other one is feeling at any given time.

The shared-room part is tricky. I like things neat and tidy. Hannah likes — well, she likes dogs. "Can't you get rid of some of these toys?" I ask whenever I trip over a stuffed dog on my way out for a run. (It makes Hannah furious when I call them toys. To her, they all have names and personalities.)

Naturally, Hannah has always begged for a dog of her own. But shortly before our eleventh birthday, she cranked up the volume. One night she brought out a magazine article about some abandoned puppies and began to cry as she pleaded with us to help her save them.

I can't stand it when Hannah cries. Why? Because, being twins, I feel her pain — literally. And I do not like to cry. I'll do anything to make her stop before I start bawling, too. I would have caved, and we would have had five or six puppies sleeping in our room that night. But Mom and Dad are tougher than I am. Mom just gave her stock answer on the dog question: "We're not ready."

"What kind of dog do you really want?" I asked Hannah later that night. "If you could have any dog in the world."

"The right dog," she said. "The right dog for me."

"A dog's a dog, isn't it?" I asked. "They all slobber and eat weird things off the sidewalk, and sniff each other's —"

"And love you, and curl up next to you, and listen to your secrets, and make you laugh," said Hannah. "Yeah, a dog's a dog. But they're all different, too. And when you meet the right one for you, you just know it." Hannah sniffled, and I was afraid she was about to start crying again. "That's why I keep bugging Mom and Dad. When the right dog comes along, I'm not going to miss out. I want to be ready."

I didn't think our parents would ever give in. But they surprised me.

"Here's what we've decided," said Dad at dinner one night about two weeks before our birthday. "Having a dog is a privilege that you will have to earn."

Hannah put down her fork and sat up very straight. "Tell me more."

"Dog points," said Mom. "You'll need to earn two hundred and fifty."

Hannah looked at me, as if I could explain. I shrugged.

"A friend of mine at work invented the idea," Mom said. "She wanted her kids to prove that they were responsible enough to take care of a pet."

"Wait, what about me?" I was beginning to feel invisible. "I don't even want a stupid dog."

Mom and Dad looked at each other. They hadn't figured out this part of the plan. "You can earn — you can earn bike points," said Mom. "Toward that one in the window at Terry's Cyclery. You said that was your dream bicycle. Remember?"

Oh, yes. I remembered. That bike was like a silver rocket, about to take off. It was shining, elegant, sleek. On that bike, I could fly like the wind. My fingers tingled. I could already feel the handlebars.

Dad raised his eyebrows. "Martha, I'm not sure a bike and a dog are in the budget —"

"Hmm," said Mom. "How about this? If Hannah earns two hundred and fifty points first, she gets a dog. If Heather gets there first, she gets the bike."

Dad nodded. "Sounds good. And to make it even more exciting, you'll have to earn the points before your birthday, or the whole thing is off."

They smiled at each other, very pleased with themselves. Hannah and me? Not so much. I'll say one thing: They were brilliant to make it a contest. Hannah may be a sap when it comes to animals, but don't underestimate her. She can be as competitive as I can. "Forget the bike," she hissed.

"Forget the dog," I hissed back. I turned to my parents. "I'm in. So how do we get points?"

Dad pushed his plate aside and pulled out an oversized pad of paper. "Meet your new friend, The Chart." He held it up. "As you'll see, points are awarded as objectives are met. There is no limit to how many points you may earn in a day or week." He grabbed a black marker and quickly added a row titled "Bike Points, Heather."

Hannah squinted at the column of chores. "Clear dinner table. Two points."

"Two points," I yelped. "That's a lot of clearing."

"Ah, but take a closer look." Mom angled the chart toward me.

"Clear table without being asked," I read. "Four points." I rolled my eyes. "Okay, I get it."

I tried to resist The Chart, I really did. Hannah and I both knew the whole thing was probably just a clever ruse to get us to do a bunch of chores. But I couldn't stop thinking about that bike.

After school the next day, Hannah ate her snack quickly, then put her jacket back on. "I'm ready," she announced.

Mom picked up a red marker and added two checks to Hannah's row.

"What're those for?" I asked.

Hannah gave me a smug look. "Mom's driving me to the shelter. It's Wednesday, remember? I get points for volunteering, plus points for being ready to go without Mom nagging me."

Hannah's a regular volunteer at the Pawley Rescue Center. I started to protest that it wasn't fair for her to get points for something she does anyway, but then I remembered the column on the chart for "Help Consuela."

Consuela is our next-door neighbor. She has multiple sclerosis and needs help sometimes, with cleaning or errands. I like helping Consuela. She's smart and funny and she used to be a world-class bicycle racer. I couldn't wait to tell her about the bike.

I would almost feel guilty for accepting points when I went to see her. Almost. I glanced again at Hannah's check marks. "I'm going next door," I told Mom. "And I'll be happy to" — I eyed the chart — "make a salad for dinner tonight. And set the table. And —" I could already picture the row of red checks growing beside my name.

Mom laughed. "Leave something for Hannah," she said.

Over the next days, Hannah and I nearly killed ourselves earning check marks. I invented a new system for loading the dishwasher, visited Consuela until she ran out of things for me to do, and helped Dad organize his nails, brads, tacks, and screws. We fought every night over who should get to set the table, and we both jumped up as soon as we'd finished eating so we could be the first to clear it. Our parents were probably wishing they'd never shown us that chart.

Honestly, I was a little tired of the whole thing myself. "After all that work, I only have a hundred and thirteen points!" I said to Hannah, a week after we'd started.

"You could always clean the basement," she said.

"Ugh. So could you," I told her. "I happen to know you only have a hundred and six." We had been neck and neck for the last few days. Cleaning the basement would push one of us fifty whole points ahead — but even with our birthday deadline looming, neither of us could face it.

Our basement is like something out of a horror movie. It's dark and damp and full of spiders, which both of us hate, and it's packed with broken furniture, old decorations, and boxes of junk.

All too soon, our birthday was only days away. We used to fight about what kind of party to have, so now we take turns deciding. Last year it was my turn. We hiked Piney Mountain and had a picnic on top. This year Hannah decided to have our party at the shelter. Mom and Dad even agreed to give us points for asking our guests to donate stuff for the animals instead of giving us presents — Hannah's idea, but I was okay with it. It's not like you usually get anything that great from other kids anyway. Lots of times it's stuff they got and didn't want and their mom put it on a shelf until they had a chance to regift it. Plus, like I said, there were those points.

When the day of the party arrived, the Saturday before our real birthday, I tried to be a good sport. I brought a bag of dog food to donate. I was friendly when I met the shelter staff. And I helped blow out the candles on our bone-shaped birthday cake. But I thought Hannah was pushing it when she asked our guests to help her walk the shelter dogs, her usual volunteer job.

"Come on, there are some brand-new dogs I'm dying to meet." Hannah led us to the dog kennels. "They just came in yesterday."

"Ooh, look at that one," our friends said as they went down the row of dogs. "Awww, so cute!"

Hannah stopped short in front of the third kennel and stared into it. I got goose bumps. I knew instantly that Hannah had just met the right dog for her.

I peered inside. The scruffy black dust mop in the cage peered back at me, its soft brown eyes almost hidden behind a wacky fringe. Those eyes . . . They looked familiar. They reminded me of someone kind and loving — Aunt Beth, maybe? I cleared my throat, wondering if I might actually be allergic to dogs. "What — what kind of dog is that?"

Hannah snapped out of her daze. "He's a schnoodle." She pointed to the sign on his cage. "A cross between a schnauzer and a poodle. His name's Tigger. Isn't he absolutely adorable?"

I shrugged. "I guess."

I looked again into Tigger's soft brown eyes. I could sort of imagine how somebody might think he was cute. I could picture him in a flowerpot or a wheelbarrow.

Hannah went back to the shelter the next day. And the next. She tried to get me to come with her, but I refused. I was not into hanging around a bunch of sad-eyed animals that nobody but Hannah wanted. I went back to helping Consuela.

The day before our real birthday, Hannah came home looking very small. Her face was pale. "They're putting Tigger's picture on the website today," she told me. "Mr. Cole says he'll get snapped up in a minute." Mr. Cole is the rescue center's director. She sat down on the hall steps. "Oh, Heather, what'll I do?" she asked. "I don't have the points. I have to let him go." Her eyes filled with tears.

I swallowed. I felt my own eyes growing moist. No! I gritted my teeth. I stood tall. I was not going to fall for it.

"Oh, Tigger." Tears began to slide down Hannah's face.

I closed my eyes and pictured myself pedaling swiftly and silently down a winding road, far ahead of a pack of other racers. Then I sighed, and let that beautiful bike roll right out of my life.

I bent down to hug my sister. "Look," I said. "If we clean the basement together, we'll each earn twenty-five points. And then if I add all my points to yours, we'll have enough for Tigger." I knew Mom and Dad would agree to that. They love it when we cooperate.

Guess what we spent our birthday doing? Oh, it was gross. Spiderwebs draped themselves across my face as I pulled boxes off shelves and carried broken toys and furniture up the stairs. When Hannah swept the floor, the clouds of dust made us both choke. We were tired, sweaty, and sore. Then I picked up one last box, and the bottom fell out. "Arrgh!" I glared down at the pile of books, cards, loose snapshots, and — what was that?

I plucked a white-satin-covered book from the heap and flipped it open. "Look at this," I called to Hannah. "You know how we hardly ever see any baby pictures of ourselves? Here's a whole album!" We sat on a broken-down sofa, under a bare lightbulb.

"Look, that's us right after we were born!" Hannah pointed to two red-faced, black-haired babies. "We looked a lot more alike when we were tiny." She turned the page.

"I can almost remember that mobile," I said. Familiar red and yellow stars dangled over our double crib.

"But who's that?" She jabbed a finger at the picture.

It was a dog. A big brown dog with soft brown eyes, lying on the nursery rug. "That's Toby," I said, without even having to think about it. I flipped a few more pages, and there he was with his head on my two-year-old lap. I knew it was me by the blond curls: by then my hair had turned lighter.

"Toby?" Hannah asked.

I shivered and tears came to my eyes. "Toby. He was soft and warm and he smelled good." The memories came rushing back. His wagging tail. The way he skidded across the floor when I chased him. His silky-soft ears, and his sweet breath. And those eyes. All of a sudden, I knew the real reason I'd offered to give Hannah my points. It wasn't because she cried. It was because Tigger's eyes reminded me of Toby's. Those eyes made me remember how it felt to love — and be loved by — a dog.

"Toby," Hannah said. "How could I have forgotten him? Of course! No wonder I've always loved dogs. Toby was the best."

I was afraid Hannah was going to start crying again, so I hurried her upstairs to show the album to Mom. She gasped when she saw it. "Toby was my dog before I got married," she told us. "When he died — oh, I was so sad. You both were, too. Heather sort of shut down, but Hannah cried and cried." She smiled at me. "You gave her all your stuffed animals to try to make her stop."

Even then, I couldn't stand to see my sister cry.

"Finally we just put this photo album away and hoped you both would forget all about Toby."

"And we did," I said. "Sort of. But I guess Hannah remembered the good parts about having a dog and I only remembered the hurt. That must be the real reason I never wanted a dog."

Mom nodded. "Same with me," she said. "But I'm ready now, and I think you are, too. I think we're ready for Tigger."

We picked him up that day. I've forgotten all about the bike — I'm too busy with Tigger. He loves to go running with me, then come back and snuggle on the couch with Hannah. Mom and Dad are crazy about him, too. It turns out that he's the right dog for all of us.

I even have a framed picture of him on my wall. Hannah took it. He's in a wheelbarrow.

Ellen Miles loves dogs, which is why she has a great time writing Puppy Place books. And guess what? She loves cats, too! That's why she came up with a series called Kitty Corner. Ellen lives in Vermont and loves to be outdoors every day with her dog, Zipper, walking, skiing, or swimming, depending on the season. She also loves to read, cook, explore her beautiful state, play with dogs, and hang out with friends and family. Visit her website at www.ellenmiles.net.

Bird Dog and Jack
by Leslie Margolis

"Make sure your father doesn't eat all of the pomegranate seeds, okay?" my mom asks as she races around the house, packing up her stuff.

"Why don't you tell him?" I ask, because I'm going to be eleven tomorrow, and I don't care about pomegranate seeds. "Or take them with you. It's not my job to nag Dad."

Mom frowns as she tucks her laptop into the front section of her wheelie bag, and then tucks her long, red hair behind her freckled ears. "You're right, sweetie. I'm sorry. May I have a hug good-bye?"

She holds out her arms and I move in close enough to smell her green-apple shampoo. "Have a good night. I love you so, so much." She squeezes me extra tight.

"Do you love me enough to get me a dog?" I ask.

She laughs even though I'm not kidding. "You're right about Dad," she says. "I'll talk to him."

"You didn't answer my question," I say as I pull away. "It's all I want for my birthday."

"Sweetie, you know it's not a good time," she replies.

I grunt as I head upstairs, taking two steps at a time. What my mom means is that she and my dad got divorced last year and they have joint custody of me. Except rather than having me switch off between their houses, we have a Bird's-Nest Custody Arrangement. And no time is a good time.

Here's how it works: I stay in one place while they Ping-Pong between the house we all used to share and their new apartments on the other side of town.

One week my mom lives here with me. The next week my dad lives here with me. They alternate being here for Thanksgiving and Christmas. On my birthday we're supposed to celebrate together like the happy family we never were. It's meant to be easy and amicable, which means friendly. And it sounds like it should be. But then there are things like pomegranate seeds, and who left the bathroom a mess, who's supposed to help me with my science fair project, and who changed the cable setup and forgot to inform the other person.

This Bird's-Nest deal is supposed to make my life easier but all it means is my mom and dad have more stuff to fight about. I so wish I had two houses like my best friend, Trevor. He's got a pool at his dad's condo complex and a giant trampoline at his mom's house. Two dogs, too: a miniature schnauzer at his dad's and a golden retriever at his mom's.

I have no pool, no trampoline, and definitely no dog.

I've had pets before, but they never last. Batman and Robin were my first.

Picture me at eight. I've got the same red hair and freckles and sticky-outy-ears I do now, except I'm shorter and even scrawnier. Also, this is pre-braces, so my two front teeth stick out.

It's my birthday and my parents tell me I'm old enough for my first pet. I'm ecstatic. Like if I could do backflips I'd be doing ten in a row. The three of us go to the pet store at the mall. I run right up to the puppy pen and pick out a small, brown guy with black floppy ears and a superlong tail that whips back and forth.

As I'm reaching for the dog — he's almost in my hands — my parents rush over to stop me. "No, you misunderstood," Dad says.

"We're getting you a fish," Mom explains, grinning like crazy, like this is actually good news.

"But I want a dog," I say, practically in tears.

"Okay, how's this? We'll get you two Siamese fighting fish," Dad says.

This intrigues me. Siamese fighting fish do not sound as good as a new puppy but they're better than nothing. It's not like I can leave the pet store empty-handed.

I pick out one blue fish and one red fish. They both have big, beautiful fins that are practically translucent.

The lady working at the pet store tells me,

"Those are both males so you'll need separate tanks because they're so aggressive."

My mom raises her eyebrows and turns to my dad. "You could've asked me before promising him two fish," she whispers, thinking I can't hear.

"Great," my dad says to the pet store lady, pulling out his wallet and ignoring my mom. "We'll take two tanks. Two sets of rocks. Two sets of food. Whatever we need."

Money changes hands. The fish are mine!

I carry one tank. Dad carries the other. Mom walks ahead of us to the car, her boot heels click-clicking fast on the sidewalk. She's not happy.

I name my blue fish Batman and my red fish Robin. I stare at them for a while. Then I call Trevor and tell him to come over. This is before Trevor's parents got divorced so he still lives down the street. He's at my place in less than five minutes.

"How come they're in separate tanks?" asks Trevor.

I explain about the fish and aggression, feeling smart and informed. I talk extra loudly too, in an attempt to drown out my parents' voices. Their fight started about the fish but now my dad is mad that my mom is Facebook friends with her ex-boyfriend, Raul.

"Let's watch them fight," says Trevor.

I flinch, thinking he means my parents. But no, he's staring at the fish.

"They need their own space," I say.

Trevor shakes his head. "They're called Siamese fighting fish for a reason. They have to fight. It's in their blood."

"Do fish even have blood?" I ask. "I think they're mostly water and tissue."

"Every living thing has blood," says Trevor. "Anyway, they probably won't even fight because Batman and Robin are buddies. Everyone knows that."

He has a good point. I dump Batman into Robin's tank.

The fish circle each other. Then they eat the food floating on the surface of the water.

"This is boring. Let's work on our hole," Trevor says.

We are digging a hole to Australia and we still have a ways to go. I follow Trevor outside.

I come home after sundown. We haven't even made it to the center of the earth, but we have made progress. I am muddy and tired. Also alarmed because Robin is missing and Batman is floating belly up in the tank.

I scream and both of my parents run up to my room. They take in the scene and my mom explains what must've happened. Batman ate Robin. Then his stomach exploded.

No more fish for me.

"Don't say 'I told you so,'" Dad barks at Mom.

Mom throws up her hands and leaves the room.

We go to Theresa's for my birthday dinner. It's my favorite pizza place and a family tradition. Except my mom and dad don't talk all night. After the pepperoni pie, my birthday cake comes out. Eight candles blaze and all of the waiters sing to me. My parents won't even look at each other. The cake should be delicious, but tonight it hurts to swallow.

For my ninth birthday my dad surprises me with a box turtle. He's asleep in his cage and I want to pick him up, but we agree to wait until he wakes up.

Turtles aren't as good as dogs, but I learn some cool things about the species: They've been around since dinosaurs roamed the earth. They can grow to be 350 pounds and live for over a hundred years. Also, in 1968, the Russians shot one into space. I name mine Michelangelo, after the Ninja Turtle. I'll wrap an orange bandanna around his head when he wakes up.

Except Michelangelo sleeps a lot. So much so that my mom intervenes and discovers Michelangelo is dead.

Yup, that's right. My dad bought me a dead turtle.

Dad takes him away and buys me a skateboard instead. I race Trevor down the driveway, fall down, and break my wrist.

We go to Theresa's straight from the hospital. My new cast itches and my parents fight, not because skateboards are dangerous — they already covered that territory at the hospital in front of the pretty nurse who winked at me and patted my knee — but because Mom says Dad is flirting with the hostess. Dad claims he's only being friendly.

On my tenth birthday my dad hands me a box. "We know you really want a dog so here's a hundred dogs," he says with an embarrassed laugh.

I am confused. The box is large. When I shake it, pieces rattle. I unwrap it and find a puzzle called Dog-a-Palooza. There are a hundred dogs pictured. Puzzles are the worst present unless you are into puzzles and I am not.

Two months later my parents tell me they're splitting up.

Tomorrow is my first birthday with divorced parents. And we can't go to Theresa's since my dad is dating the hostess and my mom refuses to set foot in the place.

I hear a car pull into our driveway and look out my bedroom window. Dad is walking up to the front door, his lumpy purple duffel bag over his shoulder. His brown hair is shorter than I've ever seen it. I can't picture his face sometimes, weeks he's gone, but when he's here it's like he never left.

Soon I hear my parents' voices downstairs. My dad is telling my mom he can't stand pomegranate seeds anyway, that she needs to relax.

Something bubbles up inside of me and I run downstairs to the kitchen.

Mom is yelling but stops, midsentence, when she sees me.

"Hey, Jack," Dad says, giving me a bear hug, then ruffling my hair. "I swear you got even taller this week."

I break away from him. "I'm not celebrating my birthday with you guys," I say.

"What?" Mom asks, confused.

"Is this because of the dog?" asks Dad.

"No!" I scream. "I don't even want a stupid dog anymore. I just want you two to stop yelling at each other all the time because you always ruin everything!"

I run outside, into the backyard to my old, rusty swing set. I am sick of the stupid Bird's Nest and I wish my parents would get regular divorced like everyone else's parents.

That's what I'm going to tell them, I decide, now that they're outside and walking toward me.

"We're sorry," Dad says, sitting on the other swing. "You're right, bud. We shouldn't ever fight in front of you."

"We'll do better," Mom says, tears in her eyes. She leans against the slide, her hands behind her back.

I want to forgive them, but I'm too mad. Also? I don't believe them.

"Hey, we have a surprise for you," Dad says.

"An early birthday present," Mom adds.

I cross my arms over my chest, hugging the chains of the swing, too. "I told you I don't want to celebrate with you."

"Well, your birthday is tomorrow," Mom points out. "And you can do whatever you want then. But right now, please come with us."

"Where?" I ask in a huff.

"You'll see," says Dad.

I roll my eyes as I stand up.

We take Dad's car. I'm in the backseat and my parents are up front. The three of us haven't been in the car together in ages and it feels weird.

Not bad, though. No one fights because no one is talking.

We end up at a place called the Pawley Rescue Center.

When we get out of the car, I hear dogs barking

but I don't get my hopes up. Inside, this tall, skinny, old guy greets us like he knows we're coming. "You must be Jack," he says to me, smiling. "The dog kennels are back here."

I look to my parents, thinking this must be a mistake. He must be waiting for some other kid named Jack.

Except Dad says, "Let's go."

He puts his arm around me and leads me toward the barking dogs.

Mom is on my other side and both my parents are smiling at each other, over my head.

This must be a trick. Maybe they signed me up to volunteer at the shelter, walk dogs that other, luckier kids will get to take home. That would be worse than the puzzle.

Except maybe not. The dogs are so cute, each in their own little enclosure.

They're in two rows, facing each other. So when I walk down the aisle there are dogs on either side of me, and they bark like crazy.

I see an older-looking Dalmatian with big pink gums. I see a brown Chihuahua with pointy ears. I see a fat little black pug, curled up on a ratty blue bed. A giant rottweiler charges the cage and barks viciously. I hurry to the next dog, a golden retriever that looks kind of like Trevor's dog, except this one keeps pacing back and forth in her cage, anxious. I see a bunch of mutts in all different shapes and sizes, and then I see her: my dog.

She's a rich shade of brown, the color of dark honey. She's got a pale pink tongue, and floppy ears I yearn to stroke because they look so soft. Her long tail curls up a bit and it wags as she stares at me.

"Um, can I see this one?" I ask, suddenly shy.

The guy who led us here nods. "Of course. Great choice, Jack. She just came in last week. She's about six months old, we think. And definitely very friendly."

"She's beautiful," my mom agrees.

The guy opens the kennel door and the dog hurries to me, sniffing my shoes and then my knees, making her way up to my face. Her breath is warm. She licks my neck and then she jumps on me. Her two front paws land on my shoulders, as if she's giving me a hug, as if we are dancing. I stroke her ears and they're even softer than I'd imagined.

"We'll have to teach her not to do that," says my dad. He puts his arm around my mom. They both watch me, smiling and smiling and smiling.

I look at them nervously. Is this really happening? I am afraid to believe.

"I'm getting a dog?" I ask.

"Yes," says Mom. "What are you going to name her?"

I look at my new dog and say the first thing that pops into my head. "Bird Dog."

Mom and Dad both laugh.

Soon we're home with Bird Dog and her new bowls and leash and food and all of the other supplies we bought at the shelter. I feel like I'm dreaming when Dad says, "Let's take a walk around the block."

Mom nods like this is the best idea she's ever heard.

I lead Bird Dog out of the car. She sniffs every single spot of the driveway, and then pulls the leash to the sidewalk to sniff there, too.

I can't believe she's going to live here with me, at the house, all the time, me and Bird Dog in the Bird's Nest.

"Let's go," says Mom.

And we walk. I'm up ahead of my parents but when I peek back they're chatting with each other and there's no anger in their voices.

I know it's not always going to be like this. There'll be more fights. But at the moment, it seems like maybe they could actually be friends.

"So can we celebrate your birthday with you tomorrow?" asks Dad. "Maybe at home?"

"We can order a pizza," says Mom.

I think for a moment and smile and nod.

We make it all the way around the block and inside, where we show Bird Dog around the house. We have dinner together, all three of us, with Bird Dog at our feet. No one fights. Mom and Dad both tuck me into bed before Mom leaves.

I go to sleep with Bird Dog at the foot of my bed. And when I wake up, she's still there.

Today I am eleven, and I already know this is going to be the best birthday I've ever had in my entire life.

❖ ❖ ❖

Leslie Margolis has written a bunch of books about kids and dogs, most famously *Boys Are Dogs* in the Annabelle Unleashed series, and *Girl's Best Friend* in the Maggie Brooklyn Mystery series. She lives in the Hollywood Hills, where she and her family enjoy hiking with Aunt Blanche, their rescue mutt.

Buddy's Forever Home
by Teddy Slater

Barkly was the first to hear it. He always is. He pricked up his ears, trotted to the door, and stuck his snout between the bars. Then he started to bark.

That's all it took. Before you could say "Kibble and Bits," all the other dogs were pressed up against their kennel doors barking like crazy. All except me.

I backed up as far as I could and wedged myself into the corner. Then I plopped down with my nose to the ground and my paws over my ears. Just in time.

The outside door opened, and three little red-headed boys came barreling through. That's when the woofing and wagging really got going, as everyone tried to get their attention. Everyone but me.

The noise was deafening:

WOOF! WOOF! ARF! ARF! BOW-WOW! A-ROOOOOOO!

You didn't have to be a dog (which, if you haven't already figured out, I am) to understand what they were saying:

"PICK ME! PICK ME! PICK ME! PICK MEEEEEEE!"

The kids flew off in all different directions, but no one flew my way. That was fine with me. Being picked was the very last thing *I* wanted. I'm perfectly happy right here at the Pawley Rescue Center.

Everyone agrees that this is a pretty cool place, but all anyone around here ever talks about is getting adopted and moving into their "forever home." I don't get it. As far as I'm concerned, this *is* my forever home and the staff and volunteers are my forever family. I love it here.

I don't remember anything about my life before I came to the Center — and from what I've heard, that's probably just as well. Let's just say I wasn't in very good shape when someone dumped me on the doorstep. But Mr. Joe, who runs the place, took me in and named me Buddy, and that's who I've been ever since.

And speaking of Mr. Joe — there he was, chasing after the kids. And right behind him was a lady who must have been the kids' mother. She had the same red hair and freckles.

The lady put two fingers to her lips and let out a piercing whistle. All the dogs stopped barking, and the boys stopped running. There was a moment of silence. Then the boys all started pointing and talking at once. And they all said the same thing:

"I want this one!"

There was just one problem. Each kid was pointing to a different dog.

The littlest boy was standing outside the biggest dog's kennel. "Isn't this one cute?" he said. "Her hair is so fluffy."

Mr. Joe chuckled. "That's Farfel," he said. "Farfel is a Bernese mountain dog, and she certainly is cute. But believe it or not, she's still just a puppy. When she's fully grown, she'll weigh more than a hundred pounds."

"No way," the mom said. "I don't want any dog that weighs more than I do!"

"Hey, look at this one," the oldest boy said, running over to Dot's kennel. "She looks just like the pups in *101 Dalmatians*."

"Dot's a beauty, all right," Mr. Joe agreed. "But she's very shy. I think she'd be happier with a smaller family."

"Well, this one sure isn't shy," the middle boy said, reaching out to pet a little black-and-white dog I didn't even know. He'd only been here for a few days.

The new dog was so excited, I thought he was going to have a fit. He slurped the kid's hand, raced around the kennel, slurped him again, and did a backflip. No kidding — a real backflip. He stopped for a moment, panting, and then went through the whole routine again.

"That's Mojo," said Mr. Joe. "He's a Jack Russell. He's full of energy and needs lots of room to run around. Do you have a big yard?"

"Nope," said the mom. "And I already have three boys who are full of energy and like to run around. I was hoping for something a little less rambunctious. How about that one?" she said, pointing to me.

"Great choice," Mr. Joe said enthusiastically. "Buddy is a Boston terrier, and you won't find a sweeter, gentler dog than him in this whole shelter."

"What do you think, boys?" the mom asked, but the kids had already moved on to Bitsy. They were all smiling and reaching out to pet her, and Bitsy was doing her best to help them. She had practically squeezed her whole head through the bars. I was afraid she'd get stuck that way.

The mom turned away from me — Whew! What a relief! — and joined the boys. "What a cute little mutt," she said. Oops! I could hardly believe my ears. No one *ever* says "mutt" around here. They say "mixed breed."

That describes a lot of the dogs here. But Bitsy's more mixed than most. She seems to have a bit of everything in her. She's fluffy like Farfel, spotted like Dot, and energetic like Mojo — well, not quite *that* energetic. In other words, she was perfect for this bunch.

I sighed as Mr. Joe led the redheads back to his office to begin the adoption process. I was happy for Bitsy. I knew she'd have a great life with that family. But I was sad to see her go. She was one of my best friends. Better her than me, though. I hope nobody ever adopts me.

Especially the picky couple Nora Clark brought by that afternoon. Nora is one of the full-time workers here. She's one of the nicest and definitely the funniest.

The couple had come to adopt a poodle puppy, but we were all out of those. The closest thing was Curly. The best you could say about him was that he was poodle-ish. He had the right kind of fur, but that was about it. His face and body shape were more like a bulldog. And you didn't have to be any Sherlock Bones to figure out that Curly was at least six years old — in dog years, that is. If he was a person, he'd be forty-two!

"I'm sorry," the man said. "I'm sure Curly is fine. But my wife has her heart set on a poodle."

"Don't worry," Nora said. "It may take a while, but we'll find you your perfect pet. In the meantime, here's a little riddle to cheer you up."

Nora always has a good joke to tell and today was no exception. As they walked away from Curly's kennel, she asked the couple, "What do you get when you cross a cocker spaniel, a poodle, and a rooster?"

The couple thought for a moment and then they both shook their heads.

"A cockerpoodledoo!" Nora said. Only she was laughing so hard that it came out "cockerpoodle-doo-hoo-hoo!" Nora always laughs at her own jokes.

The next day started off like any other day, with a delicious breakfast and a yummy liver treat. It was nice outside so we got to run around the backyard until the shelter opened for business.

I was back in my kennel taking a little snooze when Barkly started up again. The big door opened and Mr. Joe came in with what looked like two people — a man and a woman. As they walked down the aisle, though, I could see a third person. It was a young girl. She looked about nine, but it was hard to tell because she was all scrunched up, hiding behind her mother. She looked scared to death.

As they came down the aisle, I heard the mother tell Mr. Joe: "We're looking for a dog for our daughter. Tillie is very shy and we think a nice dog will be a great companion for her."

"A nice, gentle dog," the father added.

"But I don't want a dog," the little girl piped up. "I told you. I want a mouse."

"A nice, gentle, *small* dog," the mother told Mr. Joe.

"I think I know the perfect one," Mr. Joe said, stopping in front of my kennel. "Tillie," he said. "This is Buddy. He's a sweetheart, not too big, and he's quiet as a mouse! He hardly ever barks."

The little girl peeked out at me from behind her mother's skirt.

I peeked back.

Tillie had big brown eyes that looked enormous behind her thick glasses, snaggly little teeth that were partly hidden by shiny braces, and she couldn't have weighed more than a sack of kibble. In other words, she was absolutely adorable. At least *I* thought so.

Maybe because even without glasses, a Boston terrier's big browns are hard to ignore. "Pop-eyed" and "bulging" are just two of the ways I've heard them described. As for my teeth, they're an orthodontist's dream.

Anyway, I don't know if it was her looks or her personality, but something about that little girl got to me. I took a few steps toward the front of my kennel. She looked as if she was going to take a few steps back. But then a strange thing happened. Tillie came out from behind her mother's skirt and cocked her head.

I took a few more steps toward her. She took a few toward me. Soon we were so close I could smell her.

She smelled delicious.

Tillie slowly let go of her mother's hand. And now it was hanging just outside my door — right in tongue range. And before I knew what I was doing, I'd licked it. Yum!

She *tasted* delicious.

I gave her another slurp. For a minute, I was afraid she was going to cry. Her mother leaned down to comfort her. But then another strange thing happened. Tillie giggled and reached out to pet me.

And that's all it took. My fate was sealed. I never wanted another home, but now it looked like one wanted me.

But they don't just give away dogs like liver treats here. Mr. Joe and the staff do everything they can to make sure we're going to a good family.

Well, they must have decided this was a good family because a few days later I found myself in the backseat of a strange car heading into the unknown. As I watched the Center disappear through the rear window, all I could think was: *I never should have licked that little hand.*

The owner of that little hand was clearly having second thoughts of her own. Tillie sat huddled over by the door, as far away from me as possible, with her arms crossed and both hands safely tucked under her armpits.

After a while we pulled up in front of a little yellow house with bright green grass and a picket fence all around it. It wasn't the Pawley Rescue Center, but I had to admit it wasn't bad. There was lots of room to run around and plenty of dirt to dig in.

Tillie's mom turned around and smiled at me.

"Well," she said. "Here we are. Welcome home, Buddy!"

My new family did all they could to make me feel welcome. They bought me a brand-new dog dish with my name on it, all the chew toys a terrier could ask for, and a fuzzy round bed that was just my size.

But home? Nope. To me that still meant the Pawley Rescue Center. After two weeks, I was still homesick for my cozy kennel and all my pals from the shelter. Not that I wasn't making friends here. I'd already met Gus, the bloodhound next door, and Woof from across the street.

And then, of course, there was Tillie. . . .

Things had changed a lot by now and, believe it or not, Tillie was my new best friend. She kept my bowl filled with kibble and tasty liver treats. She took me for long walks and tossed a steady stream of sticks, balls, and Frisbees for me to fetch. But it was her snaggly little smile that made my tail wag. In other words, I seemed to be falling in love.

Too bad the feeling wasn't mutual.

Oh, Tillie had grown to like me, all right. She just didn't seem to trust me. Everything was fine as long as I was on the other end of a leash or running away from her, chasing whatever it was she was throwing. But as soon as I got too close, she backed away. I could tell she was still a little bit scared of me. But I didn't take that personally. Tillie was afraid of lots of things. Bats, even though she'd never even seen one. Burglars. (She hadn't seen any of those either.) Snakes. Bees. Spinach. Loud noises. The dark. And sad to say, dogs — even me.

Remember that fuzzy round dog bed I mentioned? Well, on my first night in the yellow house, Tillie's mom placed that bed on the floor right next to Tillie's bed. Tillie immediately moved it a few feet away, and that's where it stayed for the next few weeks.

Every night before she went to sleep, Tillie would stop by my bed, pat my head, and wish me sweet dreams. I think she felt braver when I was lying down. Then she'd curl up in her own bed and we'd both go to sleep — alone. I wished I could sleep next to her bed — or better yet in it — but I didn't want to push things.

And then one night everything changed. We'd both fallen asleep to the sound of a gentle rain. Suddenly a great clap of thunder woke us up. Tillie quickly pulled her blanket over her head and began to cry. I put my paws over my ears and hoped it would stop soon — for both our sakes. I'm not too crazy about thunder either. But the storm went on, and so did Tillie's crying. I kept waiting for her mom to come into the room, but I guess she couldn't hear Tillie's sobs over the storm. I could, though, and they were heartbreaking.

When I couldn't stand it anymore, I padded over to her bed. She still had the covers over her head, but one hand was sticking out. I couldn't think of anything else to do, so I stood up on my hind legs and licked it. Tillie caught her breath and her sobs slowed a bit. Then she patted my head, and I gave her another lick.

Tillie gave one last sob and then began to giggle. She raised her hand again, but instead of patting my head, this time she patted the mattress.

"Here, Buddy," she said, pulling the blanket off her head. I guess she'd decided that the storm was a lot scarier than I was. In any case, I didn't need a second invitation. Up I jumped and settled down beside her.

Tillie wrapped one arm around my neck, I put a paw on top of her other hand, and together we slept through the thunderous night.

When we woke up the next morning, the storm was over. But we were still cuddled together.

"Good morning, Buddy," Tillie said. "Isn't this a beautiful day?"

It certainly was. The sun was shining, Tillie was smiling, and I finally felt that I was really, truly home.

Forever!

🐾 🐾 🐾

Teddy Slater has written more than one hundred books for children, including *Smooch Your Pooch* and *Dottie and the Dog Show*. She lives in upstate New York with her husband, Fred. Her own beloved pooch, Barkly, often appears in her stories. He was adopted from a shelter in Sidney, NY.

Lab Partner:
An Adoption in Six Scenes
by Michael Northrop

I'm pretty sure I've been to Pawley before. It's a fairly big town and I don't live too far away, so probably, right? But I know right away that today is going to be different. This is going to be a trip I remember. Today, I'm getting a dog. My first dog ever — and I'm twelve, so that's saying something.

The light ahead of us turns red, and Mom pulls the car to a stop. I look out the window on my side at another quiet, leafy block of houses. It's pretty nice here, a lot like my town. A lot like most towns in Maryland, I guess.

The light turns green, and she steps on the gas pedal like she's afraid it might break. Mom drives like she's in an anti-race: First one there loses! I look down at the brochure for the Pawley Rescue Center again and try not to be too impatient. I've got a green light, too: I can pick out a dog, and we will adopt it. I've been asking for years, but this time I know it's true. It is my birthday present.

"Any dog I want, right, Mom?" I say.

She turns her head and looks at me. At the speed she's driving, taking her eyes off the road is pretty low risk. "Any dog," she says. "Within reason."

Within reason? What does that even mean?

"So," I start, "no unreasonable dogs?"

She smiles. Here's a secret: I think Mom wants a dog as much as I do.

We're finally at the Pawley Rescue Center. Life lesson: No matter how slow your mom drives, eventually you will get where you're going. The place is a little smaller than I thought, based on the picture, and a lot louder. Even before we open the front door, we can hear an off-key symphony of barks and yelps and yaps. It sounds awesome.

Everyone inside is really friendly. I'd tell you their names, but I get introduced to them all at once so most of that info falls right back out of my head. If there's a quiz on this later, I'm in big trouble. The lady at the front desk is really pretty, though, and the girl who shows us around is named Abby. Also, she has red hair, but that probably won't be on the quiz.

Abby is just a few years older than me. She says she volunteers here on the weekends, and she seems to know at least something about every single one of the dogs. That's pretty amazing, because there are a lot of them.

"Do you want to see the puppy play area?" she asks us, right off the bat.

Who in the world would say no to that? And sure enough, the puppy play area is a demolition derby of over-the-top cuteness. All these little fur balls are romping and rolling around. I see one black-and-gray puppy barrel into a group of three other mini-mutts and knock them over like fuzzy bowling pins. A second later, he's up on his back legs and bopping the other puppies on their heads with his front paws.

"We call that little guy Beezwax," says Abby. "Because he never minds his own business."

"What kind of dog is he?" asks Mom.

"A Siberian husky," says Abby. "Very energetic."

I like him immediately.

Next we go out back to see the yard. There are dogs in all shapes and sizes out here. Some are running around, and some are lying in the sun. Mom asks about a bunch of them. There's a bulldog and a boxer and a border collie — and that's just the *B*s! She asks me what I think about each one, but I don't know what to say. They're all pretty awesome. How does anyone ever pick just one dog? Seriously?

Then we go inside to see some dogs in the kennel. Some of them are really friendly and come right up to us, wagging their tails a million miles an hour. An enormous Saint Bernard is slobbering on Mom right through the wire door, but I've already moved on. The dog in the next pen sees me. His tail thumps the floor a few times, but he doesn't get up. His fur could not be any blacker.

"Who's this?" I say.

"Oh, that's Barkly," says Abby. "Black Lab."

Mom joins me, too. The dog's tail thumps the floor a few more times, but he still doesn't stand up.

"He's a little older, around six, we think," says Abby. "They're a little harder to place at that age, but there are a lot of advantages. . . . You know what you're getting. Less guesswork. He's a great dog!" There's something different in her voice now, but I can't place it.

"I like him," I say.

Mom looks at him a little more closely. She glances over at the Saint Bernard, then back at Barkly. "I don't know," she says. "He doesn't seem as friendly as some of the others."

She starts to move on, but I stay put. He's still looking at me, and just like that, I understand. I remember what Abby said: "harder to place." He's friendly. He's just been here longer. He's not getting his hopes up. Everyone wants the supercute puppies, or the interesting, unusual breeds. Who's going to want some six-year-old black Lab?

I guess I've been standing here longer than he's used to, because he raises his head up. Now we can both see each other a little better. And just like that, I know the answer.

"I want this one," I say.

"Oh, honey, are you sure?" says Mom. "What about Beezwax?"

I think about it for a second. Beezwax is definitely an awesome puppy. But I'm not a baby anymore, so my dog doesn't need to be either.

"Nope," I say. "This is the one."

Abby smiles really wide. Mom hesitates for a moment. When she smiles too, I know I made the right decision. I'm smiling bigger than both of them. In his cage, Barkly gets to his feet. His tail starts to really wag now. It's like he understands. We have a dog.

Barkly steps out into our backyard for the first time. He takes a few cautious steps onto the grass, and then whirls all the way around. At first I think maybe he's chasing his tail. I've heard about dogs doing that. But he's looking all around as he spins. I realize he's just taking in the full, 360-degree glory of our little square yard. It's not as big as the one at the rescue center, but he's got this one all to himself.

He spins around again, just to confirm that there aren't, like, a dozen dogs hiding behind our one skinny tree. Then he just stands there for a second, happy and maybe a little dizzy. I kneel down in front of him and start to give him the official introduction to his new place.

"Hi, Barkly," I say. "I'm Martin, Martin Benbe. You're a Benbe now, too: Barkly Benbe. It sounds pretty cool. You're going to live here now, with me and my mom. You've already met her. My dad lives here too, but he's in the navy so he's away right now. I told him about you, though, and he says he can't wait to meet you. So that will be cool, too. Anyway, this is your house behind you, and this is your yard right here. Mom asked me to ask you not to dig it up too much."

So that's my official speech. Barkly listens closely the whole time. When I'm done, he licks my face. I think that's his way of saying: "Nice to meet you; I like my yard." I stand up, and he starts sniffing the lawn like it's his job. He goes up and down in lines, as if he were pushing a lawn mower. When he gets to the tree in the center, he lifts his leg and . . . Well, let's just say I'm not sure that tree is going to make it another year.

Afterward, he follows me back into the house. I give him a biscuit, and then he decides the house needs a good sniffing, too. That's fine, as long as he doesn't decide any of the lamps need a good watering!

Barkly has a new dog bed, and he likes it a lot. He sleeps in all kinds of funny poses. Basically, whatever position he was in at the moment he fell asleep is the position he stays in. It's like he's playing a game of freeze tag with himself.

But when he's not sleeping, he follows me pretty much wherever I go. I like that. It makes everything I do seem more interesting. Instead of "I guess I'll go sit in the chair in the backyard," it's "Hey, let's go to the backyard!"

He still really likes it out there. We play fetch sometimes with an old tennis ball that is now completely saturated with drool. He's really good at starting and stopping quickly in our little yard and is downright awesome at fetch. They don't call them Labrador retrievers for nothing!

The difference is in the house. For the first few days, he walked around inside like he was in a really expensive antiques shop (an antiques shop where you get the prices by sniffing, of course). It was like he was afraid he might break something, or just a little afraid in general. But now he bounds around the house like he's in a, well, a normal house.

Mom and I are "discussing dinner options" on Wednesday night when Barkly comes tearing into the kitchen. He skids to a halt on the tile and looks at us with big, wild eyes. Then he spins around and tears right back out of the kitchen and into the living room. Mom and I both laugh. "Crazy dog," I say.

"He's figured it out," says Mom.

"Figured what out?" I say.

"That he gets to stay."

Mom and I are watching television, and Barkly is curled up next to the couch watching the inside of his eyelids. It's a little after eight o'clock, so prime time on the TV and nighttime outside. Suddenly something bangs against the corner of the house.

"Whoa!" I say, because it was really loud.

Mom doesn't say anything. She just whips her head around and looks at the spot where the sound came from. It was right by the window, but all I can see out there is dark sky and a weak glow coming from the nearest streetlight. I'll be honest, it's kind of scary. Mom hits the mute button on the remote. I look at her face. I can tell she's listening carefully. She holds up her finger to shush me.

I hold my breath and listen, but Barkly doesn't know the shush sign. About two seconds later, all Mom and I can hear is his barking. I've heard him bark before, but not like this. It's loud and rough, and it fills up the whole room. His feet are set firmly, like he's the last one in line on a tug-of-war team.

All of a sudden, he shuts his mouth, turns his head, and bolts for the front door. When he gets there, he starts barking again.

"Stay here," Mom says, and I do. Kind of. (I might trail her to the edge of the room a little.)

She gets to the front door, and peers through. There's no one there. I can't hear her let out a big sigh of relief, but I can see it.

"Good boy," she says to Barkly. "Shhhh, now. Shhhh, shhhh."

And he may not understand the shush sign, but he understands that. He stops barking and heads back toward the living room. He gives the front door one more look as he goes. It's like he's saying: "Don't make me come out there!"

"It's good to have a dog around," says Mom as she sits back down on the couch.

I try to think of something funny to say because I don't want her to think I was scared. Finally I say, "I thought navy wives could handle anything?" It's one of her favorite expressions.

"We can," she says. "But so can navy dogs."

I raise my right hand to my head and give Barkly an official navy salute. He looks over at me for a second, and then goes back to staring out that window. He'll play later. Right now, he's on duty.

Barkly and I are in the backyard, resting up from a few rounds of fetch. I'm sitting on the ground, and he sits down in front of me. Then he raises his right front paw and holds it out. I reach out and shake his hand. Well, his paw. You know what I mean.

I knew what to do because I had a friend named Jamie in the last place we lived. His dog shook hands, too. It's like a trick you can teach them. And now I'm looking at Barkly and wondering where he learned it.

It's not something I've really thought about much. I guess I haven't really wanted to. But I've always sort of wondered: How did such a great dog wind up in a rescue shelter at age six? I thought maybe his last owner was a jerk and didn't like him. But jerks don't teach tricks to dogs they don't like.

Now I'm thinking: Was it a family? Did they move? Did someone lose a job or something? Or was it one person, maybe an old guy or something? And did something happen to them? Did they . . .

Barkly stands up. He wants to play more fetch. He always wants to play more fetch. That's fine with me. I don't really want to think too much more about all that anyway. I pick up the grungy old tennis ball, soggy with fresh drool.

I guess it's not so much that I want to know the answers. It's more that I'd like them to know something. Whoever it was who gave Barkly his name and taught him how to play fetch and shake hands. No matter what happened or why they had to give him up. If they're in some other state now, or even if they're up in Heaven. I want them to know something. Ready? It's pretty simple.

I love him, too.

I pull my arm back and throw the ball. Barkly shoots across the yard like a rocket. And then he comes right back.

❖ ❖ ❖

Michael Northrop is a former editor at *Sports Illustrated Kids* and has written short fiction for *Weird Tales*, the *Notre Dame Review*, and *McSweeney's*. His middle grade novel, *Plunked*, was named to the New York Public Library's 100 Titles for Reading and Sharing. His third young adult novel, *Rotten*, is about a rescued Rottweiler. You can visit him online at www.michaelnorthrop.net.

Chihuahua Rescue!
by Randi Barrow

After old Walter fell on the icy back steps, most of us dogs knew we were in trouble. He crawled into the house and lay on the kitchen floor for a long time. Sometimes he slept, sometimes he cried. Once he called out, "One hundred and one Chihuahuas! Just like the movie!" It was something he said to everyone who visited us or dropped off another dog. That night Daffodil, Ernie, Paco, and I lay next to him to keep him warm.

The sign on his front door read: CHIHUAHUA RESCUE!!! Some of us were brought in by our owners after they lost their jobs. Others were thrown over the front gate. Me, I got lost the day my family moved. I went for a walk to look around and . . .

I couldn't find my way back. After living under an abandoned house for a week, I was grateful that someone found me and took me to Walter's. "Darndest color I ever saw," Walter said when we met. "I think I'll call him . . . Pumpkin."

He loved us and tried his best to take care of us, but there was never quite enough food or clean water. Many of us were too scared to go outside, so the floor — and just about everything else — was filthy and smelled awful. A hundred dogs were simply more than one person could handle. Sometimes people came to adopt us, but they usually left empty-handed. "We're going to think about it," they'd say, or, "I'll have to talk to my husband." I didn't care. It hurt me so much when I lost my family that I couldn't bear the idea of a new one.

Night was coming again. Walter must have been as scared as we were, because he began to pull himself into the living room on his elbows, making terrible moaning sounds until he reached the little table with the phone on it.

He was crying when he pushed a thick book off of it, saying, "What else can I do? I can't let you die!" He held it close to his eyes, shuffled through the pages, then pulled the phone off the table. "555-6431," he muttered, "555-6431." We waited, shivering and frightened, wondering what it meant. "Is this Pawley Rescue Center?" Then silence. "We need help! The dogs, my leg . . . What? About a hundred of 'em. That's right. And could you call nine-one-one for me?"

With that one call, all of our lives changed in an instant.

The knock on the door came soon after. "Mr. Tompkins? Mr. Tompkins?"

"In here." Two people scanned the room with flashlights. "Oh, my gosh!" someone exclaimed. "Look at these dogs. There must be . . ."

"One hundred and one Chihuahuas! Just like the movie," Walter said in a voice choked with sadness. Then an ambulance and several more people arrived. I ran around the house looking for Daffodil, Ernie, and Paco so we wouldn't be separated. Instead I found Spike. He was a mean dog: He enjoyed fighting the way some dogs enjoy chasing a ball. He grabbed my ankle and bit it, hard enough to make it bleed. "Just a little something to remember me by!" He yapped and ran to the rescuers as if he was the friendliest dog in the room.

As I licked my wounded leg, I realized I'd never see most of them again. "Good-bye, Walter!" I cried as they took me out to a waiting truck. "Thank you! Good-bye, everyone — good luck!"

The drive was short to the . . . what had Walter called it? The Pawley Rescue Center. They looked happy to see us, although almost everyone said we were "in bad shape." "What you need is a bath and a good home," one of them told Daffodil as she carried her off.

Someone scooped me up, saying, "You *definitely* need a bath!" I liked the way she smiled and petted me. Maybe she needed a dog. I snuggled up close to her.

"Did you see his leg?" a boy asked her a few minutes later as he helped her dip me into warm, soapy water. "That's a bad cut."

"I'll have you take him to Dr. Mehta as soon as we're done." I tried to lick her face as she scrubbed months' worth of dirt off me. It made her laugh. "Hold on!" She dried me and handed me to the boy. "He's all yours, Milo."

Milo took me to a room with a high table. "Put him down there; I'll get a muzzle on him." While the boy was very gentle, I didn't like that thing they slipped over my snout *one bit*.

The doctor was a tiny lady, with big glasses and intense dark eyes. She stuck something in my ear and called out to a girl who wrote down everything she said. "We've probably got some mites in here. Left ear has a tear that should be stitched up." With strong fingers, she felt my body from neck to tail. "Underweight, probably malnourished. Eyes could use some cleaning and drops." She pulled up my tail.

"Hey!" I cried. "There's no need for that!"

"I want a stool sample, see if we have any parasites. Now, let's look at that leg." Very carefully, she examined Spike's farewell present. "He's going to need some stitches. Start him on antibiotics." The doctor looked at me carefully and stroked my head. "He'll be okay in no time. Put him on the adoption list. How many more have we got?" And just like that, I was taken out and put in another room where they stitched and bandaged my ear and leg, and gave me medicine. I was scared, but I never felt any pain.

They fed me, then put me in a large cage with six of my friends. "Sorry it's so crowded," Milo said. Crowded? Was he kidding? He wrote something on a piece of paper and slipped it in front of the cage. "We're going to call you . . . Daryl."

Daryl? "My name is Pumpkin!" I told him.

"It's my middle name," he explained with a smile.

I plopped down next to Ernie. "Don't feel bad," he said. "They named me Brutus." I couldn't help but laugh.

"Brutus? Really? What about you, Daffodil?"

"Princess!"

"All I want is a new home," another dog said. "We heard that people will be coming tomorrow and maybe adopt us. Better get some sleep."

I curled up next to Daffodil and Ernie — I mean, Princess and Brutus — and dreamt that someone wanted to adopt all three of us.

The next morning, eager, boisterous groups of moms, dads, girls, and boys came pouring in to meet us.

"Stand up straight," Ernie told us. "Let 'em see those tails wag!" We crowded to the front of the cage, each doing our best to stand out and find a new home. Paco stayed in the back. All of his long, matted hair had been shaved off, and he wore a huge plastic cone-shaped collar so he wouldn't chew his infected paw. "I like it here," he said. "I don't want a new home."

Daffodil was the first to go. "I'm going to miss you guys!" she said as Milo reached in for her. I'd miss her too, but her new family seemed so happy and excited. Ernie was next, and then the others, until only Paco and me were left. Several times I thought it was my turn until I heard a conversation that went something like this:

"Look at this orangey one. He's cute."

"Yeah . . . but he's got bandages on his ear and his leg. That could be a problem."

"And vet bills can be so expensive."

"Hey — look at that one!" Off they'd go and some other dog would have a new home. By late afternoon I was disheartened, and my tail hurt from all that wagging. Then two women stopped in front of our cage.

"I can't believe Thanksgiving is next week," one said.

"I got off easy. All I have to bring is a pumpkin pie."

Did she say *Pumpkin*? My ears went up, my head snapped around.

"Hey, they're talking about you," Paco whispered. "Stand up."

"I make them from scratch. First I buy a pumpkin, cook it, and grind it up myself." Paco and I stared at each other in disbelief. A pie? From a *Pumpkin*? "Oh, look, this little dog might be a good one." I backed up slowly.

"I go a little pumpkin crazy at Thanksgiving: pumpkin cookies, pumpkin bread, pumpkin ice cream, pumpkin mousse. . . ." My teeth chattered, my whole body started shaking. I had to get out of this place before she thought of any other recipes to put *this* Pumpkin in.

"Hide in back of me," Paco said, "behind the collar." But it was too late.

The pumpkin-eating lady said, "I think I like this one best."

"Let's see them all first," her friend said, "then we'll decide."

"*You* are in trouble," Paco said, when they'd gone. "What are you going to do?"

I was so upset. I liked it here, I liked the people, and now because of one pumpkin-crazed person I was going to have to leave. "I'm going to run away."

I circled my cage twice. The door latched on the outside, but they opened it to put our food in. That's when I'd make a run for it. It was almost closing time so dinner would be soon.

"Where will you go?" Paco asked.

"I don't know. Back to Walter's?"

"You'll never find it. And they took him away in an ambulance. You'd be alone."

"I'll figure it out. No one wanted me anyway."

Paco looked like he was sad for me. "Good luck, buddy."

Soon Milo appeared with two bowls of food. I didn't want to get him in trouble, but I had to leave. "Here you go, guys." He opened the cage door, and before he could put the bowls down, I took off.

"Hey! Come back!"

I remembered where the front door was: to the right, down a hall, left to the lobby. My leg was sore from the stitches and the bandage made it hard to run, but my timing was perfect. A family of four was just coming in the door. The dad was holding it open for his toddler.

"Look!" the mom cried, pointing to me as I zoomed past them.

Milo cried, "Daryl! Daryl!"

It was dark and cold outside. Where should I go? Where? Several cars were parked off to my right. I ran under the first one, then the next, until I was under the one farthest from the front door. Before I could decide what to do, a car pulled in next to me. I held my breath.

The driver got out, then opened the back door on the passenger side. What was that sound?

"Don't cry, *mija*," he said softly. "It's going to be okay." I inched closer so I could hear everything.

"But, Papa, I don't want anyone to see me!" She sniffed and cried softly.

"It's only a patch on your eye. Think how much better you'll see when it's off!"

"I hate it. And I hate my glasses." She cried some more. "I'm ugly now."

He knelt down. I could have reached out and touched him. "Listen to me. *Rosita bonita* — isn't that what I've always called you? Beautiful little Rosa?"

She gasped for air. "Yes."

"Your patch will be gone in days. And glasses make people look smart!"

"Not mine."

"Yes, yours. They shout, *I am a smart girl who loves to read!*" She laughed. "Give me a hug, *Rosita la bonita! Rosa la inteligente!*" She laughed some more, and sniffed her tears back.

"Come on. Your *abuela* said she'd make tamales for this new dog of yours."

Abuela? Tamales? I couldn't believe my ears. I hadn't let myself think of my family's *abuela* who loved me so much before I got lost. Every Sunday we sat together while she made tamales.

This new family was my destiny, and I'd almost missed it. I had to get back in. But how? Just slip out from under the car and let them see me? No, they might think I'm a stray. I ran back to the car closest to the front door. Surely Rosa would enter the building first, and then her dad. I'd sneak in after them and run to my cage. They'd see me and know I was the dog for them.

Except — the door was locked. The dad knocked. Finally a man opened it. "It's okay. Come on in," he said, and locked the door behind them.

I was dumbfounded. "But . . . you're my family! I know it," I called out. If I didn't get in there right away they might adopt another dog. The wrong dog.

I ran to the front door and started barking. No one came. I glanced around the parking lot. It was made up of small pebbles. I quickly sucked one into my mouth, and spit it at the glass door. It made a pitiful little ping. I tried a bigger one, and got a slightly louder ping. No one would hear that, no one would come to investigate.

I inched closer until my nose touched the glass and started to howl. Rosa would go home with someone else. I whimpered. I'd been *so close* to finding the perfect family. Just as another whimper shook me, I heard the door open. "There you are!" Milo exclaimed, bending to pick me up. "I thought you were lost!" As he carried me in, all I could think about was Rosa. *Where's Rosa?* We went down one hall, turned, and almost ran into the pumpkin eaters.

"Oh, look!" one of them said. "Is he still available?" I leaped out of Milo's arms, landing hard on the floor, hurting my bandaged leg.

I ran, up one hall and down another, until I found them. Rosa was staring into a cage, looking sad.

"Rosa!" I barked. "I'm here!" And limping, barking, and whimpering, I ran, and with all my strength I jumped as high as I could, and . . . she caught me. In both arms.

Never had I licked a face, neck, or ears so enthusiastically, letting her know just how much I was meant to be hers.

She giggled and held me close. Her dad looked amazed. "Papa, look! He likes me. And he has bandages. Two of them!" She laughed as I put my paw on her shoulder and nuzzled her cheek.

Her dad ran his hand over my head. "He could be the one."

Milo came running up. "You found him."

"He found me," Rosa said. Milo reached out for me, but Rosa turned away and shook her head. "He's ours."

Later, when we were driving home, Rosa said, "I don't think Daryl is his name. He needs just the right name." I nestled in closer to her as she studied me. "I think I'll call him *Calabazito*."

Her father laughed. "It's a little long, but good."

That's when I knew I was really home. My old *abuela* used to call me the same thing. *"Ay, mi calabazito,"* she'd say.

In English? "Oh, my little pumpkin."

❀ ❀ ❀

Randi Barrow is the author of *Finding Zasha* and *Saving Zasha*. When dogs entered her life a dozen years ago, the effect was profound, and dogs have continued to inspire her writing. Randi lives in Los Angeles with her husband and their Chihuahua-mix companion, Manuel. For more about Randi, visit her website at www.randibarrow.com.

Foster's Home
by Jane B. Mason & Sarah Hines Stephens

The last thing Evelyn Maybeck needed was another creature to care for. Everyone in Pawley knew she kept her three-bedroom place stuffed with critters that needed looking after. They were mostly kids from Social Services, but also the occasional dog or cat from the Pawley Rescue Center, weekending classroom rodent, or down-and-out friend.

Evelyn didn't turn anyone away, because while her house was small and stuffed to the rafters, her heart was enormous and could expand to fit. If her heart had a tag, it would read: ONE SIZE FITS ALL. And it would actually be true.

Whenever Evelyn got a call from Social Services she welcomed the new foundling with an open door, open arms, and little regard for the extra work it created. She knew that her job, providing basics — clean clothes, enough food, a warm bed, a ride — was easy compared to the emotional curveballs a kid in transition was fielding. Bitter divorces, legal problems, hospitals, painful pasts — these were the things that shattered families, pummeled children, and dropped them on her doorstep. Evelyn did all she could to soothe their bruises with warm food, kind words, and a safe place to stay.

So while it was not unusual to see Evelyn balancing a baby on her hip while she looked over long division homework and unpacked groceries to start dinner, it was unusual to see her generous backside sticking out from under her peeling porch. But that was exactly what it was doing on a Monday morning in May.

"Come on out of there," Evelyn coaxed the mud-covered something cowering in the corner. "I won't hurt you."

"Won't hurt," Kirby, a mop-headed toddler, echoed at her heel. He held out a crust of toast temptingly.

Evelyn, Kirby, and Jora, who was ten, had been aware that something was under the porch for several days. At first they thought it was Captain Jack — the one-eyed cat Evelyn had taken in a year or so back. Jora thought perhaps Jack had returned for more tuna. Only the frightened beast was too big to be a cat. Whatever was hiding under the stairs was large enough to shake the whole porch when it trembled against the rail post, and frightened enough to keep the porch vibrating almost constantly.

"All right, have it your way. I'm in no hurry." Evelyn backed out slowly, hips swinging. When she stood up, her knees were dark with damp spring mud and she had a smudge on her cheek. She brushed at the spots, rubbing in the dirt, but there was no time to change. Jora needed to get to school. Kirby was out of Goldfish. And Evelyn was picking up a new charge today — an older child. Thirteen, they'd said. So much could happen before a kid reached thirteen.

Evelyn told Jora and Kirby that they'd need to be kind. That they'd need to be extra patient. All three of them — four — would need some time.

Jora nodded. She remembered when she was first with Evelyn.

After Kirby dropped his toast by the opening under the stairs and waved good-bye to the mystery creature, Jora strapped him into the car seat in the rusting Volvo. She tugged on the seat belt, worrying about who would sit with her at lunch. About how things would go with a new foster sibling. She hoped it would be a girl. A girl would be nice. Evelyn wondered what time they'd be back — maybe the scared critter would be gone by then.

When the Volvo pulled back into the narrow drive it was nearly dark. Kirby was sound asleep in his car seat, a half-eaten apple browning in his hand. Jora gathered her books into her backpack and started to unbuckle the three-point harness.

"I'll get that, plum cake," Evelyn said tiredly. "You get to your homework." It was late. Dinner wasn't made. Evelyn was worn out, and worried about her newest charge. They'd been together for five hours, but Charlie, a boy, hadn't said a single word. He just followed, at a distance, while they went to the grocery store, picked up Jora from school, and stopped for underwear, socks, and other essentials (Evelyn guessed at the size). And now that they were at the house, he made no move to get out of the car.

Jora trotted to the stairs, which seemed to start the porch shaking again. Evelyn was so distracted by the new boy that she'd forgotten about the quivering mystery creature. Kirby, groggy on her shoulder, dropped his leftover apple over the rail. "Here, kitty." He yawned before flopping his head back down and burrowing further into sleep.

"Evelyn?" Jora asked softly, glancing back toward the car. "If it's a cat, could we keep it?"

Evelyn smiled. She loved it when the kids in her care used the word "we," like they were a family. Because "we" were all they had for the moment. "We'll have to see," she told Jora. "Whatever's hiding under there might need help. Remind me to call Joe at Pawley Rescue Center to come take a look — if we can get it to come out."

Jora scrambled back down the stairs to peer past the lattice into the dark, her backpack sliding. "I see eyes!" she cried.

So did Evelyn. Charlie had emerged from the Volvo, his eyes peeking out from under the beanie he wore pulled down to his lower lashes. They were a bright hazel color, like gold-flecked gingerbread. They brightened for the slightest instant, then went vacant. A pang of tired worry spread through Evelyn's chest.

"Careful now," Evelyn warned Jora. Cornered creatures could lash out, and an excited kid, even one as cautious as Jora, could seem loud and intimidating. "Speak softly. He's probably scared."

Jora nodded and whispered encouraging words into the darkness. Charlie took a few steps forward and stood, half looking, for a long moment.

"Wanna see?" Jora waved him closer.

Charlie lowered his gaze and slunk back to the car.

Evelyn watched the skinny boy go and shifted Kirby higher onto her hip. Sometimes it took days for a foster child in her care to trust her. Sometimes weeks. Sometimes they never did.

While Charlie shifted from one foot to another by the car, Evelyn thought that maybe this time she'd made the wrong choice. Maybe thirteen hard years were just too many. Jora was still crooning and Kirby was getting heavier by the second, so she took him inside and laid him on the couch. The little guy had missed his nap and it was too late to be dozing, but she couldn't bear to wake him. She covered him with a tattered quilt and went back out for the groceries, looking kindly at Charlie but not saying anything. After seven years of fostering, Evelyn knew that some kids needed time and space to think, especially the older ones. She just hoped it was enough.

Charlie came inside for dinner — grilled cheese sandwiches and tomato soup — but kept his jacket on and didn't eat much. And when supper was over he disappeared back to the porch while Evelyn settled Kirby into bed and Jora at the table with her math notebook.

Standing at the sink with a tub full of warm suds, Evelyn watched the boy through the window. He had half a sandwich in his hand — the half she thought he'd eaten — and held it out beside the porch. He stood very still and stayed quiet. Even as a dark snout began sniff, sniff, sniffing its way out from underneath, Charlie stayed perfectly still.

Evelyn held her breath as the dog's mouth opened. In the yellow porch light she saw a purplish tongue. Dark lips pulled back and gently, so gently, the dog put his teeth on the sandwich, as if it might shatter. Charlie didn't move as he released the offering. The nose disappeared, and Charlie stood. Several minutes passed before Evelyn pushed open the screen door and called the silent boy to bed.

Charlie shuffled inside without glancing at Evelyn. She showed him his bed, the clothes she'd gotten for him, the new toothbrush on the sink. He didn't even nod.

Tomorrow I'll call Joe, Evelyn told herself as she folded laundry. Joe would know what to do about the dog. She smiled, thinking of Pawley Rescue Center and the Cole family. Yes, Joe knew about strays. He would know what to do.

The next morning, Charlie wasn't in bed. Kirby noticed first. "Charlie? Charlie? Charlie, where you go?" he asked, wandering the house in footy pajamas.

Evelyn's heart began to race. Maybe she'd pegged the boy wrong. Maybe he was a runner. But when she opened the front door to shout for him, she saw the top of his knit beanie over the railing. He was sitting cross-legged beside the hole under the porch. A damp snout with a black licorice tip stretched out of the dark, just touching his jean-clad leg. Evelyn exhaled and eased the screen door shut so it wouldn't slam. The lunch meat she'd bought the day before was gone from the fridge. She made peanut butter sandwiches instead, herded the children into the Volvo, and dropped the older two at school. Charlie climbed out of the backseat without saying good-bye.

After "Wheels on the Bus" sung three times through (not skipping any verses) and five readings of *But Not the Hippopotamus*, Kirby went down for a nap, at last. Evelyn peeked into Charlie's room on her way down the hall. The socks and underwear sat on the dresser, still in their bags, untouched. She eyed the dishes in the kitchen sink, ignoring them while she filled a plastic bowl with water and stepped onto the porch. Pressing her palm against the wooden rail, she felt the smooth wood and nothing else. The porch wasn't shaking, and Evelyn felt a pang, thinking the dog might be gone.

"Hello down there," she sang softly. "Are you thirsty?" There was no movement as she set the bowl next to the opening, but a tiny whimper let her know the stray was still there.

Evelyn went inside and picked up the phone to call the rescue center. Joe was busy, which was not hard to imagine, and Evelyn left a message with the friendly girl at the desk before adding kibble to the shopping list.

They hadn't eaten dinner when Charlie's caseworker called. Evelyn and Jora set the table while Charlie was on the phone.

When Charlie came out from the bedroom his nose was red. Evelyn couldn't see his eyes as she took the phone in exchange for a bag of dog food and a metal bowl. She knew better than to ask questions. She knew that, to Charlie, she was still a stranger.

The boy walked straight out the front door. He clumped down the stairs, sounding heavier than his slim frame could possibly be. Jora ran after him, anxious to cheer him up, but Evelyn held her back. "Come on, plum cake," she said. "I need help with the dishes. Will you rinse?"

That night the dog emerged from his hiding place. He slunk up the stairs and onto the porch, standing at the edge, his feet ready to run. Charlie watched silently, patiently, for a long time. Finally he opened the door. The licorice snout quivered in the narrow opening for a moment. Then the pooch stepped into the hall, his broad head hanging below skinny shoulders.

"Stinky!" Kirby announced, holding his nose. The dog smelled something awful.

Out in the light the animal looked like a mash-up of every canine who had ever lived in Pawley, and a few that hadn't. Smaller than a Lab, bigger than a beagle. He was black and brown and gold with two stripes on his low-hanging tail and a brindle back end. His eyes were dark and deep, and his ears flopped. His paws were too big for his body.

Jora thought she heard Charlie whisper something to the dog as he followed him to his room. She wondered if she imagined the flicker of a smile on Charlie's face.

The next morning when Charlie and Jora went to school, the dog went back under the porch. He slipped out silently with one of Charlie's dirty socks in his mouth, and when Evelyn looked in on him later he had it curled around his nose. Charlie's new bag of socks had finally been opened.

After school the dog greeted Charlie with a baleful bark. He wagged and wagged and the stink rose off him, prompting Jora to come running with a bottle of baby shampoo.

"Not yet," Evelyn said, though a bath was a good idea, and the thought of all the bedclothes that now needed to be taken to the Laundromat made her cringe. She held Jora back. "They're settling in."

They all settled until the sound of a horn in the drive, about an hour later, made everyone jump. Kirby smashed his face against the screen door, which made Jora laugh and smash hers on the other side.

"Joe." Evelyn could have slapped her forehead when she saw who it was. She had forgotten all about him. She waved and smiled, stepping off the porch to meet him.

"I got your message about a stray. I was just headed back to the rescue center and thought I'd see if I could give him a lift." He smiled, and Evelyn's stomach clenched. A stray.

His eyes crinkling at the edges, Joe took a moment to say hello to Jora and Kirby, still playing with the screen. Evelyn glanced back. She scanned the small yard. No dog. No Charlie. "Mighty nice of you, Joe." She smiled back. "Only . . ."

"Only what?" he asked. He had a gentle face. Patient.

"Only, it's gotten complicated." Evelyn sighed and rubbed at her eyes. She stepped to the far side of the porch, the one without the opening, and motioned with her head. Through the lattice they could both see the dog and the boy, crouched together in the cobwebs.

Joe ran his hand through his coarse graying hair. He nodded, eyes still crinkling. "So he's not a stray after all."

"Not after all," Evelyn agreed.

"You sure you have room for another foster?" Joe asked.

"Foster!" Kirby parroted from the doorway.

Under the porch the dog barked, like he'd understood it all.

"Foster."

Evelyn startled. It was the first time she'd really heard Charlie's voice. He and the dog crawled out from under the porch and Charlie stood up.

"Foster? Is that your name?" he asked with his hands on his knees, looking into the dog's face. The dog barked again. Charlie pushed his hat back just enough so he could see . . . a little . . . and looked at Evelyn. "He can stay?" he asked timidly.

Evelyn nodded, tired but happy. "Sure, he can stay. Looks to me like Foster's already home."

❧ ❧ ❧

Jane B. Mason & Sarah Hines Stephens live in Oakland, California, but not in the same house. They spend their time, which seems to keep

120

disappearing on them, writing, cooking, gardening (mostly Sarah), and swimming (mostly Jane), while attempting to keep up with their respective children, husbands, and dogs, who don't usually disappear but are increasingly hard to keep up with. They are the authors of A Dog and His Girl Mysteries (woof!), and several Candy Apple titles, including *The Sister Switch* and *Snowfall Surprise*.

Big Dogs
by C. Alexander London

Simon knew the bully's weapons all too well: There was the wedgie and the purple nurple, the swirlie, the noogie, and the punch-buggy dead arm (no punch-backs).

Those were the most common tortures, but there were others that didn't have names, like the one where they splashed water onto his pants so it looked like he'd wet himself, or when they called out "Thorry, *Thhhh*-imon" in high-pitched voices just because he lisped sometimes.

But that was all about to change.

After today, no one would dare mess with him, because his parents were taking him to the Pawley Rescue Center to get a dog. And he meant to pick out the biggest, baddest, meanest-looking dog he could find. He was going to put a spiked collar on it and he was going to teach it to growl at anyone who made fun of him.

The police used big German shepherd dogs to chase down criminals. Maybe he'd get one of those and call him Axl. Or a pit bull — people were always scared of pit bulls. Maybe he'd get a big pit bull and name him Spike.

No, that wouldn't do. Spike started with an *S*. Too risky. Axl wouldn't work either. There was a chance he'd say "Ack-thel," and then everyone would laugh at him, mean-looking dog or no.

Maybe Diablo, which was Spanish for "devil" and didn't have any *S* sounds in it. He figured his parents wouldn't let him just name the dog Devil, but Diablo was multicultural. His parents would like that.

"Diablo," he said out loud to try it out on his tongue. "Di-a-blo."

"What was that, honey?" His mom turned around from the front seat.

"Nothing," Simon said.

"Are you excited?" She smiled at him. "Big day! I'll never forget when my parents took me to the kennel to adopt my first dog. He was a big mastiff, taller on his hind legs than my sister and me. We named him King Kong."

"Cool," said Simon, adding a mastiff to his list.

"He *was* cool," said his mother. "And the sweetest dog you ever saw. He was huge, but he'd never hurt a flea. Mostly he just slept and snored and snored and snored."

"You don't think it's sweet when *I* snore," his father said as he merged into the exit lane.

"Well, you aren't as fuzzy and cute as King Kong was." His mother laughed.

"I think I want a pit bull," said Simon. What was the point of having a giant dog if it was just fuzzy and cute?

"Simon, remember," his father said, "you aren't picking a new toy. A dog is a living thing. You can't choose just based on looks. In fact, I think it's the dog who chooses you, rather than the other way around. Let's just wait and see which dog wants to be a part of our family."

When the car stopped at the squat brick building, Simon jumped from the backseat to run inside.

"Remember," his father called after him. "It's the dog who chooses you."

"I know!" Simon groaned, already picturing Diablo with his slobbering jaws and massive fangs. He wondered if the shelter sold spiked collars.

But an hour later, when they left the shelter, Simon wasn't thinking about spiked collars. He was thinking how unfair it was that the dog his parents said had "chosen him" was nothing like the dog he'd pictured.

This dog was a short, squat, black-and-brown, smush-faced French bulldog, with stubby legs and big bugged-out eyes and a little pink tongue that hung out the side of her wheezing, panting, grunting mouth. That's right: *her* mouth.

His big, tough dog wasn't only not big and tough; she was a girl.

Also she already had a name, which was nothing like Diablo.

Beatrice.

Who named a dog Beatrice?

She did have slobbering jaws, though. She slobbered a lot.

"I think she's adorable," his mother cooed.

"She's ugly," Simon grumbled.

"She's so ugly that she's cute!" his mother replied. In her crate, Beatrice stared out at him with her black bugged-out eyes. Her panting mouth took up half her head, like a giant grin, and the way she wheezed as they loaded the crate into the car, Simon was sure the dog was laughing at him.

The animal shelter had told them that Beatrice was up-to-date on all her shots, that she was housebroken, and already knew a few basic commands like "sit" and "stay." They couldn't tell Simon whether or not she knew any tricks.

"Why don't you take her outside and find out?" Simon's father suggested before dinner. "You two could play and get to know each other."

Simon crossed his arms and scowled. Beatrice, now out of her crate and sniffing around the kitchen, looked up at him, wagging her tail.

Except she didn't really have a tail.

Instead, her whole backside wagged back and forth, so much that it knocked her little legs around under her and she skittered from side to side as she wagged. Her front paws danced back and forth, and the whole time she stared up at Simon with her dark bug eyes and she snorted. Her smushed nose made the loudest series of snorts and wheezes Simon had ever heard. She wasn't a dog, he decided. She was an alien.

He could already imagine how the other kids would pick on him for this.

But he had promised to walk the dog if they let him get a dog, so he clipped her leash on and they stepped outside.

"Come on, alien dog," he told her as she bounded across the yard, each of her steps like a pounce. He prayed no one would see him. He prayed no one would make him say her name out loud.

They made their way across the lawn and turned onto the sidewalk. The dog tugged ahead, trying to drag him, but she wasn't nearly strong enough so she just tilted sideways as her paws scraped at the sidewalk. With every step she took, she made more weird noises . . . and not all of them came from her front end.

When he turned from his street onto Maplewood Drive, he saw Patrice Grayson and her little brother playing basketball in their driveway. They looked in his direction, and Patrice said something to her brother. He laughed and pointed at Beatrice. Simon tugged her in the opposite direction.

Beatrice didn't even notice the pointing. She sniffed at every bush and investigated each mailbox. She stared at Simon and panted.

"Would you do your *thing* already?" Simon groaned, but Beatrice would not be hurried. She stopped to cock her head at the birds singing in Mrs. Quinto's magnolia tree.

Suddenly she made the craziest noise. She warbled. Or cooed. It definitely wasn't a bark or a growl like a normal dog.

But she wasn't warbling at the birds or cooing at the magnolia tree. She was warble-cooing at the two figures who stepped out from behind Mrs. Quinto's magnolia tree at that moment: Mason Pratt and his dog, Maximus.

Mason was an eighth grader, which he thought made him the boss of the neighborhood. Maximus was a Doberman pinscher, a tall, black-and-brown dog with rippling muscles, a long brown snout, and a narrow head with ears that poked up like devil horns. He was the kind of dog Simon had dreamed of. He was terrifying.

"Hey, *Thhhh*-imon," Mason said.

Simon ignored him and tried to walk past with his head held high, but Beatrice had other plans. She used all the might in her little legs to drag him toward Mason and Maximus.

"Is that supposed to be a dog?" Mason sneered, as his own dog cocked his devilish head at Beatrice and let out a low, belly-rumbling growl.

"Beatrith, no!" Simon shouted, and then he saw Mason smirk. He blushed.

"Beatrith?" Mason laughed. "Its name is *Beatrith*?"

"Be-a-trice," Simon said slowly, making sure he got the *S* sound right.

"That's not what you said," Mason told him, grinning.

"I —" Simon felt the hot pressure of tears behind his eyes. His mouth twitched as shame burned through him. And then, with a lunge, Beatrice broke free from his grip and charged across the lawn toward Maximus, letting out a string of high-pitched almost-barks as she bounded toward the big dog on her stubby little legs. Her leash slithered in the grass after her like a snake.

"Arf! Arf! Arf!" she squealed.

"Grrrr," Maximus warned, and Simon imagined he could feel the earth shake with the growling. He wanted to cry out, to call her back, to dive forward and grab the alien dog with the name he couldn't say right, but his mouth felt like it'd been filled with sticky syrup and his feet felt like they'd been glued to the ground.

The hair on the Doberman's back bristled. His lips curled to show sharp teeth glistening with slobber. Beatrice stuck her nose in the air right beneath those shining teeth, her bugged-out eyes fixed on Maximus, whose own had narrowed to cruel slits. The big dog reared back, snapping his leash from Mason's hands and knocking the boy down.

"Max! No!" Mason called out.

Beatrice lowered her face to the ground, sticking her front paws out and raising her backside into the air, and then she flung herself at Maximus as he flung himself at her. When they collided, Beatrice landed on Maximus's head, her legs splayed out on either side of his ears, like a hat. The big dog shook and sent the little French bulldog twirling through the air. For a moment, with her tongue flapping sideways from her mouth and her paws stretched out in front of her, it looked like Beatrice was flying. Just before she hit the grass and rolled, Simon could have sworn her slobbery lips bent up into a doggy smile.

In an instant, Beatrice popped onto her feet and bounded straight back to Maximus.

"Arf! Arf! Arf!" she challenged him. This time Maximus raised his backside in the air. But instead of springing on Beatrice, or swallowing her whole in his fearsome mouth, he flung himself sideways, dodging her as she leaped at him. He whacked her with his big black paw and she flew again across the lawn, popping back up with an "Arf" as soon as she'd stopped rolling. Maximus was ready for her next charge and rolled and bounced around her, as she leaped and barked around him.

"They're — they're — playing?" Mason said, his mouth hanging open.

Simon could only nod, watching his tiny, chubby, big-headed dog play with the most ferocious dog in the neighborhood.

"But . . . Max doesn't like anyone!" Mason objected.

As if disagreeing with his master, Maximus barked once and rolled over onto his back, letting Beatrice jump over him and climb across him like he was a playground jungle gym. She licked the underside of his face.

Mason and Simon stood there, side by side, watching as Maximus batted Beatrice around and Beatrice bounced back, all snorts and warbles.

"Your dog's pretty tough," Mason said.

"Yeah," Simon agreed, casting a sidelong glance at the boy. "She is."

He waited for an insult to follow, but none did.

When the dogs had tired themselves out, Maximus lay on his side, panting, and Beatrice lay curled between his front legs, using his big neck for a pillow. Her mouth was wide open and she snored. When Maximus tried to move, she growled. The big Doberman lay still again, not daring to disturb his little friend's rest.

Mason and Simon both laughed.

"She's such a bully!" Mason chuckled.

Soon Simon's pocket vibrated and he took out his phone. "Dinnertime," he said. "I gotta go." He approached the sleeping dogs and picked up Beatrice's leash. Maximus raised his head from the grass, then looked to his master and whimpered.

"Come on, Max," Mason said.

As they walked half a block side by side, the big dog next to the little one, it looked like Mason was about to say something, but instead, when they reached the corner, they went in opposite directions without another word.

At lunch the next day, Patrice Grayson had Simon cornered with some of the other girls. They were all bigger than him. Patrice leaned across the red plastic tray he held. One good whack and she could knock his two slices of garden vegetable pizza casserole to the floor.

"I saw your weirdo dog, *Thhhh*-imon," she said to him. "Was the pet store all out of real dogs?"

"She's not from a pet thtore," Simon answered.

"What's a pet thtore?" Patrice laughed, and her friends giggled behind her.

"Pet. Store," Simon said carefully, studying the casserole on his tray. "I got her from a shelter."

"Oooh! A shelter! Aren't you heroic!" Patrice cooed. "You *rescued* her, just like a knight in shining armor. Is she your princess now?"

"I . . ." Simon wanted to say something back, but he could never find the right words.

"You aren't going to defend your princess's honor?" Patrice asked.

"I . . ." he said again, and then he thought of Beatrice rolling over Maximus, getting knocked around and bounding back for more. Where'd the little dog find that kind of courage? Could she teach it to Simon? He didn't figure he could just start wrestling Patrice and her friends. He'd end up with an atomic wedgie. Beatrice was lucky. You couldn't give a dog a wedgie.

Still . . . Beatrice wouldn't let fear stop her from playing. It was worth a try.

"I *wanted* a princess," he said. "But I accidentally rescued the troll under the bridge instead."

Some of the girls snickered. Patrice wrinkled her forehead. She hadn't expected Simon to joke. She didn't seem to like that her friends were laughing.

"Actually," Simon added, "a troll wouldn't snore as loud as Beatrith does."

The girls laughed, and they definitely laughed with him this time, not at him, even though he'd missed the *S* sound.

Patrice balled her fists and her friends stopped laughing.

"Hey!" someone yelled. Everyone turned to see Mason Pratt, holding his own lunch tray, with his eyes fixed on Patrice. "Don't make fun of rescue dogs," he told her. "My dog's a rescue dog, too."

"We were just making fun of *Thhhh*-imon's weird little —"

Mason shook his head, and with just that little shake, Patrice fell silent. "His name is *Simon*," Mason told her as he looked her friends in the eye one by one. "And his dog is cool."

Patrice frowned. "Whatever," she said and led her pack of friends away. One of them looked at

Simon and smiled as she passed. It was not a cruel smile. She'd liked his joke.

When the girls had gone, Mason looked at Simon, up and down, the way Maximus had looked at Beatrice.

"Thank you," said Simon.

Mason shrugged. "Wanna play with our dogs after school?"

"Uh, okay," Simon said.

"Cool." Mason smiled. "I wonder if we could teach them tricks together. They could be, like, a comedy act. Max and Beatrice."

"Yeah," Simon agreed. They spent the rest of lunch period coming up with ideas for their dog act. It'd be a lot of work to teach Beatrice and Maximus what to do, and Simon worried his dog was too small for some of their ideas.

"The size of the dog doesn't matter," Mason said. "Little dogs are just as good at stuff as big dogs. Maybe even better sometimes."

"I'm lucky she chose me to come home with, then," said Simon. "I think it's the dogs who pick the people, you know, not the other way around."

"Yeah," agreed Mason. "Dogs are pretty good at that."

❧ ❧ ❧

C. Alexander London is the author of Dog Tags, a series of books about dogs in wartime, as well as the Accidental Adventures novels. When he is not writing, he can usually be found walking around New York City talking to his dog. Visit him at www.calexanderlondon.com.

Package Deal
by Marlane Kennedy

Rudy Martin first asked for a dog when he was four years old.

"Maybe one day, but not now," his mother replied.

"When will one day be?" Rudy asked.

"When you are old enough to be responsible and take care of a dog," his father said.

"How old is 'spon-sit-a-bull'?" he asked. He didn't know exactly what responsible meant, but he knew he needed to pay careful attention to his father's answer.

"When you're twelve," his father said.

"Yes, twelve is a good age to get a dog," his mother agreed.

Every birthday from then on, Rudy reminded his parents of their promise. Before blowing out the candles on his cake, he would say, "Only seven more years before I get my dog."

"Only six more years . . ."

"Only five more years . . ."

Until today. Today was June 15 and Rudy was turning twelve! And his parents, true to their word, were taking him to the Pawley Rescue Center, where Rudy would finally be able to pick out a dog of his very own.

When they arrived at the rescue center, Rudy could hardly contain his excitement. He had waited eight long years for this! And though he knew he would be getting a dog, there was still the thrill of surprise involved. Would his dog be big or little? Shaggy or sleek? He couldn't wait to find out!

Rudy dashed ahead of his parents, alongside the hydrangea bushes in full bloom lining the sidewalk, and burst through the doors of the brick building. He ran up to the front desk, his face flushed with excitement.

"Where's the fire?" a tall woman with short blond hair asked, grinning.

"No fire," Rudy said. "I'm just here to adopt a dog!"

"Well, I'm Nora and I'd be glad to help you," she said.

When Rudy's parents caught up to him, Nora explained they'd need to fill out an adoption form, but that they could take a look at the dogs first. She led them to a large room with rows of roomy kennels. "Are you interested in a puppy or an older dog? Any size requirements? A specific temperament?" she asked.

"Maybe a younger dog with some energy to play, but sort of laid-back, too," said Mr. Martin.

"A dog that has already been house-trained would be nice," Mrs. Martin said. "And past the chewy-young-puppy stage."

"What about you?" Nora asked Rudy. "Any suggestions?"

"Nope. I love all dogs," he said. And he truly did. He desperately wanted to take home each and every dog they passed.

Like that big, shaggy Goldendoodle.

"That's Delilah," Nora said. "Her coat will need lots of care. She'll need to be brushed regularly and you may also want to budget in trips to the groomer, but she is an amazingly friendly and lovable dog!"

Rudy stood in front of the Goldendoodle's kennel. He imagined throwing a ball for Delilah to fetch in the backyard.

Then there was a Chihuahua who quaked and crept to the front of the cage with big, sad eyes that said, "Take me home, please!"

Rudy wanted to hold her in his arms and give her a hug. He imagined her curled up on his bed, snuggled next to him.

There were mixed breeds and purebreds — some lunging against the cage doors, urgently demanding attention, while others sat patiently waiting for a hand to reach in with a pat. His heart ached for each one. How could he choose?

"You seem awful quiet," Nora remarked to Rudy as they ended the tour of the room. "Cat got your tongue? Or should I say *dog*?" She laughed. "Aren't there any here that you like?"

"I like them all," Rudy said. "That's the problem."

"You could adopt more than one. How about forty?" Nora joked.

"Oh, no. We can only afford one," Mr. Martin said, even though he knew she was teasing. "I've researched the cost of food and vet bills!"

"I admire you for that," Nora said. "We promote responsible adoptions. When people get in over their heads, the dogs suffer or end up back in shelters."

Rudy saw a classmate of his across the room. Sophia Cole was busy putting a beagle back in his kennel enclosure. Sophia's father ran the Pawley Rescue Center and she'd often told Rudy about helping out.

"Hi, Sophia," Rudy called.

"Hi, Rudy!" Sophia walked over to the group. "Nora, I just passed Dad in the hallway a minute ago and he told me he needs you back in the office when you have a chance."

"Okay. Then how about you show Rudy and his parents to the outdoor play area?" Nora asked. She smiled at Rudy. "There are about ten more dogs you haven't seen yet back there. Maybe one will stand out and make your decision easier."

More dogs! Rudy thought that would only make things harder. He was already overwhelmed. He followed Sophia out to the bright sunshine and the fenced-in play area.

"Oh, gosh, look!" Rudy said, pointing.

A long-eared basset hound bowed down in a playful stance, wagging his tail, while a tiny mutt with a squashed face ran up and pounced on his shoulder before dashing away. The basset sprang up and chased after the little dog, then quickly bowed down again with a friendly bark, asking for another round of pounce and chase.

Rudy laughed, amazed at how gentle the stout basset was with the little dog.

"That's Bagley," Sophia said. "He's about two years old and a real character. Makes us laugh all the time. He and the pug mix, Lena, came to the shelter about the same time last month and they are pretty much inseparable. Do you want to go meet them?"

"Sure!" Rudy said.

"Those two aren't a package deal, are they?" Mr. Martin asked.

"No," Sophia said. "Sometimes if dogs have a long history together and come from the same home, we do require a joint adoption, but that isn't the case with these two. Bagley was a stray found wandering the streets. And Lena belonged to a nice older gentleman who had to go to a nursing home."

When Sophia let the Martins inside the fenced-in area, all of the dogs came rushing forward in a frenzy of excitement over having new company. Bagley, however, sauntered over and then immediately collapsed at Rudy's feet, showing his belly. He wanted a belly rub. Rudy happily obliged.

In the middle of the chaos of dogs clamoring for attention, Rudy was drawn to Bagley. Was it his velvet ears? The soft, floppy skin around his neck and mouth? There was just something about him. "Are you a good boy?" he asked.

Bagley leaped to his feet, tilted his head back, and answered, "Arrrrooorooo!" Rudy swore that all of the dog's loose, hanging skin was gathered into a huge smile. Lena sat beside him and let out a dainty bark, as if to say, "Yes, he's a good dog!"

"I found my dog," Rudy said, grinning.

When Rudy and his family pulled into their driveway, Mrs. Kolinski, their neighbor, was out watering her flowers. She was a widow in her seventies who had become something of an extra grandmother to Rudy. Since Rudy's real grandparents lived far away, it was nice to have Mrs. Kolinski around. She came to his basketball games and his band concerts, where he played the trumpet. It worked out well. Though Mrs. Kolinski had grandchildren, they lived in another state, and she didn't get to see them very often either.

Mrs. Kolinski turned off the water and wandered over. "Did you find a dog?"

At that moment, Bagley hopped out of the car, his new green leash dangling from Rudy's hand.

"Got my answer!" Mrs. Kolinski said. "Oh, it will be nice seeing a dog around. We always had a couple of them when my kids were growing up. But I've got a bad hip now and I'm afraid I couldn't handle the regular walks — especially in the winter. Plus, I don't want to deal with the hassle of boarding the dog when I go to visit my grandchildren. I'll just borrow this fella from time to time if that's all right." She patted Bagley on the head.

Bagley wagged his tail so hard, the whole back half of his body swayed back and forth.

"What's his name?" Mrs. Kolinski asked.

Rudy was told he could change the dog's name if he wanted to, but he liked the name the shelter staff had given him. "Bagley," he said. "That's my dog's name."

It sure feels good to say "my dog," Rudy thought. He had waited a long time, but Bagley was worth it!

That evening Bagley sniffed around the yard, chased a tennis ball, performed a duet by howling right along as Rudy practiced on his trumpet, greatly enjoyed his dinner, and blissfully soaked in all the love Rudy showered upon him. But the next morning, Bagley was a different dog. He only ate a few bites of food. He did not want to chase a ball. All he wanted to do was put his paws on the front windowsill and stare out at nothing.

Occasionally he would let out a whimper or a moan and then would curl up on the floor.

"Could Bagley be sick?" Rudy asked his mother.

"I'm not sure. Maybe we should take him to the vet," she said. Rudy noticed his mother looked worried, too.

But at the vet's office, Bagley got a clean bill of health.

"He's in tip-top shape," the vet told the Martins. "But he's definitely looking a little down. Maybe he's depressed. Big life changes can do that to a dog. If his mood doesn't improve in the next few days, bring him back."

On the way home, Rudy's mom said, "What on earth could poor Bagley be depressed about?"

"Lena," Rudy said. "Remember his friend? Maybe he misses Lena."

"We could take him to visit the rescue center tomorrow to see if he perks up," his mother said. "Then we'll know for sure. I'll call Nora Clark and let her know we're coming."

The next day, during Mr. Martin's lunch hour, he, Rudy, Mrs. Martin, and Bagley made the trip to the rescue center. When they entered the building,

Bagley immediately lifted his droopy, hanging head. Nora met them at the front desk and told them Lena was not her usual self either. "Since Bagley left, she's no longer lively Lena. She's become lackluster, lonely, and lost Lena."

Bagley pulled at his leash, practically dragging Rudy down the hall.

"I think he's ready to get the show on the road!" Nora said. "Let's go!"

When she pushed open the door to the kennels, Bagley immediately headed for Lena's crate. "Arrrrooorooo!" he sang, and his tail started wagging a mile a minute. Lena jumped up against the cage door, barking like crazy.

"Let's take them to the outside play area," Nora said.

Once in the freedom of the grassy yard, the two dogs romped and played. What Rudy saw could only be explained by two words: pure joy. It made him happy to see Bagley happy, but it also made him sad. "Now what?" he asked.

"Maybe," his mother said gently, "Bagley and Lena need to go to the same home."

"I think that may be for the best," Nora said.

She gave Rudy a sympathetic look. And instead of her usual quick, joking manner, her voice became soft. "They've bonded. Sometimes that happens — though usually it's with dogs that have been raised together."

"We can't take them both," Mr. Martin said. He put his hand on Rudy's shoulder. "You understand, don't you?" he asked.

Rudy nodded. There was a lump in his throat. He swallowed hard.

"Maybe we can look for another dog," Mrs. Martin said, attempting to sound cheerful. "Did you have any other favorites?"

Rudy shook his head. "I can't pick out another dog. Not right now. Maybe another time." From the moment he saw Bagley, he felt like that was his dog. That they were meant to be. He turned to leave the fenced area and suddenly Bagley was trotting beside him.

"Arrrooorooo," Bagley howled, giving Rudy a "come on and pet me" look. But Rudy couldn't bring himself to stoop down for a proper good-bye. It would be too hard. He just kept walking without looking back.

The car ride home was quiet. When they pulled into the driveway, Rudy spotted Mrs. Kolinski sitting on her front porch swing.

"How's handsome Bagley?" she called out to her neighbors as they got out of the car.

"We had to take him back to the rescue center," Mr. Martin said.

"Oh, my!" Mrs. Kolinski left the porch swing and walked over. "He seemed so nice! Did something happen?"

"Not really," Rudy's mother said. "He just left behind a friend — a little pug mix — and it made him awfully sad. He wouldn't eat. Wouldn't play. But when he saw his friend again, the old happy Bagley returned. So we decided the dogs need to be together. The rescue center is hoping to find someone to take them both."

"A pug mix? The first dog I ever had was a pug! She was just the sweetest thing. I loved her so. But . . . well . . . enough about that. I know how disappointed you all must be that it didn't work out," Mrs. Kolinski said.

"I think I'll go inside now." Rudy's head slumped down as he walked toward the house. He didn't want to talk about losing Bagley. It hurt too much. He was almost to the door when he had a thought. Eyes wide, he ran back across the yard.

"Mrs. Kolinski!" His words came out fast. "Would you get a dog if you had someone to walk it every day? And someone to keep the dog when you visit your grandchildren?"

Mrs. Kolinski looked confused at first, but then smiled. "And who would that be?" she asked.

"Me!" Rudy exclaimed.

"Well, I suppose so. That is, if that dog happened to be small. Maybe a pug mix? And maybe one that has a basset hound friend living next door?"

"Mom? Dad?" Rudy asked.

"Well," his father said. "We do share a backyard fence with Mrs. Kolinski. Maybe we could put in a doggy door so the dogs could play together."

"And then Bagley and Lena could spend time together every day!" Mrs. Martin said.

Within minutes, Mrs. Kolinski joined Rudy and his parents on the trip back to the Pawley Rescue Center. And it was love at first sight. Lena and Mrs. Kolinski seemed meant to be together. In one fell swoop, two dogs found loving homes.

As time passed, Rudy proved himself to be, as he said when he was four, "spon-sit-a-bull." He took both dogs on regular walks and played with them in their shared backyard. And when Mrs. Kolinski went to visit her family, Rudy dutifully fed, watered, and took care of two dogs. But it was worth it, because he finally had a dog to call his own. A dog that slept on his bed and fetched his ball and helped him practice his trumpet by howling right along. But the thing that Rudy loved best about Bagley?

He was one very happy dog.

Marlane Kennedy is the author of *Me and the Pumpkin Queen, The Dog Days of Charlotte Hayes,* and the forthcoming series Disaster Strikes. She lives in Wooster, Ohio, with her husband, daughter, a moose of a chocolate Lab named Carl, and his best friend, Ralphy, a shaggy white mutt adopted from a rescue group.

The Heart Dog
by Elizabeth Cody Kimmel

Henry didn't mean to eat the pie. It was all just a horrible misunderstanding. He had gone into the kitchen to *look* at the pie, and to *smell* the pie. He may have even put out his tongue a little, to get just a hint of the *taste* of the pie.

But now he had crumbs in his whiskers, and the pie tin was on the floor. And there wasn't any more pie in it.

It was Bad to go to another dog's house and eat things. And though there was no dog living in this house, Henry knew he had done something Bad. Now Granny Lee might scold him in the Loud Voice.

Granny Lee had told Henry to be Good when she put him in the car that morning. She told him again to be Good when the car hummed and purred for a very long time while Henry watched things whiz by the window. She told him to be Good when they stopped at a big green house and the man, woman, and small girl came out of the house. Granny Lee kept her hand on Henry's collar when she hugged the little girl, who seemed to want to touch Henry but wouldn't.

Be Good, Henry.

And now he had been Bad. No one had told Henry that, but he knew it just the same.

He would take the pie tin and bury it. But to bury something, Henry needed to find a Digging Place. The Digging Place would be in the yard. Yards were on the other side of doors to Go Out. But where was the door to Go Out in this house?

The red wood square in the kitchen smelled like a place to Go Out. Henry picked up the pie tin and carried it there. At Granny Lee's house when he sat by the door to Go Out, she would come and open it. But Granny Lee did not come.

She was in the big room, talking to the man and woman. He could hear her voice saying his name.

"I've had Henry for six months now, and I couldn't ask for a better friend. He's such a good dog. I do wish you'd adopt one for Alice — it would be so good for her, and she can't be frightened of ALL dogs!"

Henry heard the words Good Dog, and his tail drooped. Good Dogs did not Go Out to bury pie tins with no pie in them.

He turned around. The small girl had come into the kitchen. She watched Henry. Henry watched her.

He wagged his tail and took a step toward the girl, but she jumped back. She was afraid of him. Henry knew that when a human smelled scared, especially a small human, it was best to go away and do something else. He turned back to the door and scratched it. Then he looked at the girl again. She looked at Henry, and she looked at the pie tin in his mouth, and she looked at the door to Go Out. Very carefully, she inched toward the door. She never took her eyes off Henry, and he never took his eyes off her. The girl opened the door a crack, then scurried away.

Henry nudged the door open with his paw. Moments later, he was standing in a yard. But this yard was made of sidewalk stuff. There was no Digging Place. Henry could not bury the pie tin here.

As he stood wondering what to do, Henry heard his name. Granny Lee was calling him from inside. Henry felt so Bad at that moment, he could only think of one other thing to do, which was something else Bad. He jumped the small gate, landing on the sidewalk with the pie tin still clutched between his teeth, and began to run.

Henry did not stop running until he found a street where no cars were moving. He stood trying to pant without putting the tin down. Nothing looked familiar. Nothing smelled familiar. He could not hear Granny Lee calling his name anymore.

But then he heard something else — a high, sharp bark in the distance. He put his ears up and listened hard, then he ran toward the sound. He saw a low building surrounded by lots of good

Digging Places, and the air was full of the irresistible smell of dogs. Lots of them. Holding his tail a little higher, Henry ran toward the building.

Now Henry's eyes could see what his nose had already told him. Next to the building was a wonderful yard with a fence around it — an Outside for playing. And it was filled with puppies of all shapes and sizes. Henry could remember being in an Outside like this once before. A large man had taken him from a street like the one he was on now — a street with no familiar smells, no Soft Places or Kibble. That had been a cold time, when his stomach was always empty and nobody rubbed his head. But the man took him to a place with many other dogs, and one day Granny Lee was there. She had rubbed his head and looked into his eyes and called him her Heart Dog, and after that every day was Home.

Henry trotted up to the fence, where a puppy was making a nice hole in the earth, big enough to fit a nose inside. Henry barked, and the puppy's head flew up. She stared at Henry, her face, nose, and mouth covered with delicious-smelling dirt. She wagged her tail hard, and put her ears up.

Henry wagged his tail hard too, and stretched his head toward the fence to get more of the good smell of puppy mixed with dirt.

Between all the sniffing, Henry heard the sound of a human voice.

"Daisy, no digging! Come here, girl! What have you — hey, who's this?"

The girl walking across the yard toward the fence was neither small nor large. As she approached the fence, Henry lifted his nose and sniffed curiously. This human was not afraid — she smelled of kindness and Squeaky Toys. Henry liked her, and he put his ears up and wagged his tail enthusiastically. The kind girl laughed.

"He's a beagle just like you, Daisy! And isn't he a handsome boy! You wait right there, buddy, I'm going to come around and get you, okay? You wait."

Henry knew how to Wait; in fact he was sometimes very good at Wait, but not all the time. But Henry very much wanted to get closer to the kind girl. He could often guess when a human might be particularly good at rubbing ears or scratching tummies. This girl, Henry knew, would be good at both.

Moments later a door in the building opened, and the girl came out carrying a leash.

"Good boy!"

Henry wagged his tail even harder than before and sat as still as he possibly could, happy to hear the word Good.

"Nice boy. That's right — I'm not going to hurt you."

The kind girl was right next to Henry now. She rubbed his head with one hand and clipped a leash to his collar with the other. Henry made a little whimper of happiness because it felt so good to have his head rubbed.

"Come on inside, buddy, and we'll get you sorted out. You look lost!"

Henry wanted to roll over and show the girl his tummy, but Inside was fine, too. Maybe there would be a Squeaky Toy, or a Bone, or a Soft Place to sleep.

Inside smelled very clean, with traces of many different dogs, and some Not Dogs, too. Henry trotted next to the kind girl, then waited patiently while she opened a door that led Outside for playing.

"How do you get along with other dogs, buddy? I bet you're very friendly. Do you like to play?"

Henry barked when he heard Play, and was delighted to see the digging puppy race over to meet him. They touched noses and sniffed and wagged tails. The puppy pounced and whirled in a circle, and Henry pounced, too. The kind girl laughed and unclipped the leash.

"You like Daisy, don't you, buddy? Good boy — I bet you looked just like her when you were a pup!"

Henry and Daisy pounced and scrambled on the grass. Another, larger human had joined the girl Outside, but Henry did not take much notice of the man. He was too interested in playing with Daisy.

"Yeah, Rob, he was right outside the fence, saying hello to Daisy. The phone number on his tag isn't local — it might be an Annapolis area code. Maybe he's got a microchip. I'd say he's definitely lost, though."

Daisy butted Henry with her nose and then wriggled onto her back like she wanted to have her head rubbed and her tummy scratched. Daisy was a good pup, but she needed her own human, so she could be a Heart Dog.

That made Henry think of Granny Lee. His human. And how she had found him in a place like this once before and after that everything was Home. Henry stopped midpounce and looked through the fence to the grassy place where he had first sniffed Daisy. Standing there now was the small girl from the green house.

Henry froze. His tail stopped wagging. His ears drooped slightly. He remembered that before the nice girl called him Good and rubbed his head and brought him to this Outside playing place, he had done something. Something Bad. And there was the pie tin lying right in the grass where Henry had left it, and the small girl had picked it up.

"Hi! Hey, you don't happen to be looking for a lost dog, do you? We just found a beagle! If you hang on a second, I'll come around and let you in so you can get a better look at him!"

It had felt so wonderful to be Good. Henry did not want to be Bad again, but his whiskers still smelled very faintly of pie, and Granny Lee would know it because she always knew things even when Henry thought he had done a thing nobody could ever know. Ignoring Daisy's yaps, Henry ran to a bush in the corner of the yard and squeezed underneath it. He would stay here, where no one could see him, and though he would still not be Good, he wouldn't be Bad either.

"Where did he go? You said your name was Alice, right? I'm Abby, and I work here at the rescue center. I promise he's in this yard somewhere, Alice. Don't worry."

Henry stayed crouched low under the bush, but he pushed his head out far enough so his nose and his eyes could find out what was happening.

There was the small girl, Alice. She was standing very close to the door to Inside, and though the other dogs kept right on playing and left her alone, Henry knew she was extra afraid.

Unlike the other dogs, Daisy did not ignore Alice. She trotted right over to her and sat down and stared at her very hard. Henry knew Daisy was hoping with all her heart this little human might want to rub her head or scratch her tummy, or tell her she was Good. And suddenly Henry forgot about wanting to be Good and not wanting to be Bad, and all the pictures and smells in his head were replaced by his first Home memory when Granny Lee had found him in a place like this, and Henry had looked at her very hard. The way Daisy was looking at Alice. And Henry knew instantly that Alice was supposed to be Daisy's human, and after this, every day should be Home for Daisy, too. Most dogs know right away when they find their human. But sometimes humans are a little slower to recognize their Heart Dog.

Alice was shaking her head and backing closer to the door Inside. If Henry came out of his hiding place, Alice would see him and tell the kind girl — Abby — about the pie. But Henry had to make Alice see that she was Daisy's human. There was only this chance, just now, while Daisy was still close enough to touch Alice. Henry knew that once Alice put her hand on Daisy's soft head and looked into her liquid brown eyes, her fear would be gone and her heart would fill with love. The way Granny Lee's heart had filled when she put her hand on Henry's head.

"Oh, there he is! Is that him, Alice? Is that your granny's beagle?"

"Yes — that's him, but can we go inside, please, and call Granny from there?"

Henry knew he had to pounce at just the right moment. He took a few running steps, launched himself into the air, and landed just where Daisy was still wagging her tail hopefully in the grass. As Henry collided with the puppy, the impact sent her tumbling head over paws in a hedgehog roll, right onto Alice's feet.

"Daisy!" Abby cried, and Alice made a small sound like "Oh!" and put her hand out to push the puppy off her feet.

Then Alice froze, and Henry froze, and Abby froze, and for a moment every dog in the yard froze, too.

Alice's hand was lightly touching the top of Daisy's head. After a moment, Alice bent down slightly. And Henry could see that Alice was looking right into Daisy's big brown eyes. And just like that, the way the air changes when a new bag of kibble is ripped open, everything changed. Alice did not smell Afraid anymore. Alice smelled the way all humans did when their Heart Dog has found them.

Abby led Henry inside to an office. He sat quietly, and after some time he heard a familiar voice in the hallway. The door to the office opened, and there was Granny Lee. Henry flung himself at her, wagging his tail and licking her hand and jumping up just a little. Granny Lee did not scold him at all.

"Oh, Henry, thank goodness! Thank you so much, Abby — I can't tell you how relieved I am to have Henry back!"

"Well, you have your granddaughter to thank for that. She told me she saw him jump the fence in her yard and she followed him all the way here, then told us how to call her house to find you. She's outside — she's absolutely fallen in love with one of our puppies."

"Alice? Playing with a puppy? That doesn't sound like my granddaughter!"

Tail high, Henry followed Granny Lee and Abby back Outside. And though Granny Lee smelled very Surprised at what she saw there, Henry was not.

When Granny Lee finally clipped Henry's leash on to take him to her car, Alice had Daisy held tightly in her arms. When Henry jumped into the backseat, Alice climbed in carefully next to him, still holding Daisy tight. Alice held Daisy that way all the way back to the green house, and Henry knew there would be many things to do there. Bowls would be chosen and Soft Places to sleep would be made and heads would be rubbed and tummies scratched and from now on every day for Daisy would be Home.

And very likely, nobody would ever think to mention the pie again.

Elizabeth Cody Kimmel lives with her family in New York's Hudson Valley. She is the author of many books for children, including *Legend of the Ghost Dog*, *Balto and the Great Race*, the Suddenly Supernatural series, and *Paranorman*. She spends her spare time reading, hiking, singing in the choir, and trying to communicate telepathically with her beagle.

Farfel

by Allan Woodrow

I turned off Grove Road, ran up the walkway, and dashed into the shelter's reception area, twelve minutes later than usual. I waved to Aunt Nora, who was sitting behind the front counter, like always. She was the reason I got to run around the place. It was practically my second home. She threw me a smile. "What kind of market does a dog hate?" she asked me.

"A flea market," I said, rolling my eyes. Aunt Nora frowned. "You told me the same joke last week," I explained.

"I need new material," she said with a small nod. "And you're late."

"I know. We have a new crossing guard at

school. He's slooooow." Anytime a car came within a mile of the street we had to wait. And wait. I'm all for safe street crossing, but he would have to chill. There's safe, and then there's paranoid.

I pushed my way through the doors that led into the back kennel.

In my rush, I nearly ran over Mr. Cole, who runs the Pawley Rescue Center. He's always reading papers and walking, so he doesn't always pay attention to where he's going. I sidestepped just in time to avoid a serious crash.

Now *he* could use a crossing guard.

"No running, Quentin!" he warned me.

"Sorry!" I said, slowing down just a little. "Excuse me!"

"Good afternoon, Quentin," said Dr. Mehta, the head veterinarian. She was holding a hamster. You wouldn't think a hamster would end up at a rescue center, but I guess everyone needs a place to stay sometimes, even little guys. "He's waiting for you. You're late."

"New crossing guard," I explained, hurrying to the back.

Rob Matthews had been working at the shelter as long as my aunt Nora. He was already holding Farfel when I got to the back. He handed her to me. "Hey, man. You're late."

I nodded. I'd really have to set that new crossing guard straight.

I held Farfel and her face lit up like a thousand holiday lights. I bet mine did, too. I've been stopping by the shelter to play with her every day since she came in, just over a month earlier. She had been only a few weeks old when she was abandoned in front of the shelter one night. She was so small and so quiet! She was super shy around everyone except me. When I came in, she'd start yapping and bouncing.

She was practically mine, even though she lived at the shelter.

Farfel jumped up and threw a flurry of excited licks all over my face. "Calm down, girl," I said, giggling.

I carried her to the back play area. It was a small, carpeted room just for puppies like Farfel so they could run around without any worries about getting injured. I scratched her white furry chest and then rubbed her sleek black back. Farfel was a Bernese mountain dog, so she was black and white, with some rust-colored markings above her eyes and to the side of her mouth. Bernese mountain dogs grow to be pretty big, but Farfel was only fifteen pounds. She wouldn't hit her full weight and height until she was two or three. Still, she would probably be close to eighty pounds before she was a year old.

"I have a surprise for you," I said. I pulled out the new rubber bone from my backpack. I bought it from the pet store the other night with birthday money. My birthday was in two days, but Grandma sent her check early.

I really wanted to drop off the bone before school but that would have meant skipping class and Mom would have killed me. I was already on thin ice, too — our teacher had handed our history tests back. I got a C. Mom would be disappointed. She got straight As in school. She was practically a genius.

"I'm going to the game tomorrow!" I told Farfel, although she knew that already. I had only mentioned it about a zillion times. Mom promised to get us tickets to see the Washington Wizards. They play only about an hour away, but I'd never been to a professional basketball game before. It was going to be the best birthday ever.

Going to the game was the only present I wanted. Well, not really. But it was the only present I wrote on my birthday list. Two years before I had asked for a dog and instead Mom bought me sweaters. Then the past year I had asked for a dog and Mom bought me pants. There was nothing worse than getting clothes for a gift. Mom was going to buy me clothes anyway — it wasn't like she would let me go to school naked. So getting clothes for my birthday was practically the same as getting nothing.

I wasn't making *that* mistake again. I didn't need any more clothes. So this time I wasn't asking for something that pooped or made a mess. That's what Mom said is the only thing dogs were good for. You know, sometimes Mom didn't know so much for being a genius and all.

Besides, going to a basketball game would be great. Not dog-great, but still pretty awesome.

🐾 🐾 🐾

When I got home, Mom was working, like usual. When she heard me walk in, she came out of her office and smiled. Her smile always made me smile. "How was school?" she asked.

"Same old," I said with a shrug. I just hoped she wouldn't ask me if I got any tests back.

"Did you get your history test back?"

The lady was psychic. "Um. Maybe."

"You didn't do very well, did you?"

"How did you know that?"

"Moms know everything."

I told you she was a genius. I showed her my test and she shook her head and grumbled. I hoped she wouldn't punish me. A birthday should be like an automatic Get Out of Jail Free card — you should be exempt from punishment for anything.

"We'll talk about your test later. I should ground you," said Mom. "But your birthday *is* coming up." I swallowed my smile. I didn't want Mom to think I was gloating. "And we do have a game to go to tomorrow night."

She held up the Wizards tickets and handed them to me. I felt their sharp edges and was careful not to crease them. I didn't want to ruin them or anything. I would have jumped out of the chair and given Mom a monster hug and told her she was the greatest mother in the world. Except I was almost twelve years old, and twelve-year-olds don't do that sort of thing. Still, I smiled so wide it was like my mouth was hugging her, if you know what I mean.

Mom's cell phone rang. She looked at the caller ID and hurried back to her office. That's what she did when she got important phone calls. It also meant I probably wouldn't see her again until bedtime, if then. Luckily, I was an expert frozen-pizza-for-dinner maker.

"What kind of dog tells time?" asked Aunt Nora.

I rolled my eyes. "A watchdog. Come on. I think you told me that one when I was like five years old."

My aunt laughed. "I really do need new material."

I rushed back to see Farfel. I narrowly avoided smashing into Mr. Cole, who had his nose pressed against some papers as he walked. "Quentin!"

"Excuse me!" I shouted back. "Sorry!"

I hurried past Dr. Mehta. She held a black cat with white spots. "Good afternoon, Quentin," she said.

"Hi, Dr. Mehta."

When I got to the back, Rob was just taking Farfel out of her cage. She and I went to the play area, where Farfel licked and jumped on me and we rolled around a bit before playing tug-of-war with her new bone. "Tonight's the game!" I told her. I was sure Farfel was as excited as I was. Farfel whipped her head around to get the bone away from me, but I wasn't letting go that easily. "I'll tell you all about it tomorrow," I promised, struggling to keep my grip on her toy.

Back home, Mom was working. She didn't even come out to say hello. When I stuck my head in her office she was on her phone and shooed me away. Mom worked way too hard, if you asked me. I knew she has to work for two ever since Dad left, but you have to save some time for fun. I made myself a cheese sandwich for a snack, but I was only halfway through eating it when Mom came out. She looked tired — even more tired than usual. She threw me her smile. But the smile was only in her mouth and not in her eyes — they didn't get wrinkles on the sides like they're supposed to — so I knew the grin was fake. "How was school?"

"Same old," I said with a shrug.

Mom sat down at the table. Her smile was gone. I looked at her nervously. "Quentin, I have a big project that's due tomorrow. It's taking a lot longer than I thought."

I continued to eye her warily.

"There's no way I can go to the game tonight," she continued. "I'm going to have to work. I'm sorry."

It felt like Mom had socked me in the gut. "But we have tickets."

"I know."

"But you promised."

"I'm sorry."

"Maybe I can go by myself? Or with a friend?"

"That's not possible. It's too far away and too last minute to find anyone to take you. I'm really sorry, Quentin."

"It's not fair!" I yelled.

"I know you're upset."

"You don't know anything!" I yelled back before storming out of the room and up the stairs, then slamming my door shut.

The next morning when I got ready for school, Mom was still working. I think she might have been in that room all night. She always got me doughnuts on my birthday. It was sort of a family tradition. But there were no doughnuts today. Not even a card. I poured myself some cereal, ate in silence, and went to school. So much for this being my best birthday ever.

I ran down Grove Road to the Pawley Rescue Center right after school. That new crossing guard needed to be replaced, that's for sure. At one point we didn't see any cars, but someone was riding a bike — a bike! — and he made us wait. By the time the bike passed, the light had changed and a hundred more cars appeared.

But at least I could hang out with Farfel for a little bit. It would mean my birthday wasn't a total loss. I'd probably get home and find out Mom had run out and bought pants for my gift. If I even had a gift, since we weren't going to the game anymore.

Aunt Nora wasn't behind the counter when I came in, which was strange. So I went through the doors without her usual bad joke.

I pushed through and I almost slammed into Mr. Cole. I avoided him just in time. "Oh, Quentin, hold on —" he began.

"Sorry! Excuse me!" I didn't stop.

Next I passed Dr. Mehta, who was holding a rabbit. "Oh. Quentin, wait a moment —" she said, but I was running late so I rushed past her, too.

Rob wasn't at the cage to hand Farfel to me. So I slowed down just a little bit when I got there. I skidded to a stop. "Hey, Farfel!" I shouted. "Sorry I'm late."

But the cage was open and empty — except for the rubber bone I had given her, which sat alone in the back. I pulled it out and stared at it, confused.

From behind me, a hand went on my shoulder. I figured it was Rob, waiting to hand Farfel to me. I needed a little birthday hug from her. But he wasn't holding anything.

"Where's Farfel?" I asked.

"Farfel was adopted today," he said.

"What do you mean?"

"We rescue animals and put them up for adoption. And —"

"But Farfel was mine." I mean, I know she wasn't mine *officially*. But she was mine *unofficially*, and that was practically the same thing.

"But you'll never guess —"

I didn't hear the rest of what he said. Farfel was gone! She was the only one who would have understood how important last night was to me. She would have made me feel better — better than anyone else ever could.

I headed to the door. I needed to get out. I needed air.

"Wait a second —" yelled Rob as I dashed to the door. I didn't slow down and I almost ran into Mr. Cole again.

I didn't even say, "Excuse me."

When I got home, the house was quiet. Mom was out. There were no presents or cake, just a house as empty and sad as I felt. I still held Farfel's rubber bone. I stared at it and turned it over in my hands. A rubber bone without a dog was like a birthday without any presents.

I then heard something from the garage.

It was probably a squirrel or something. Last year one made its way into our garage and attacked our garbage cans. It made a mess. I sighed and walked past the mudroom to the garage, ready to shoo away whatever animal had come in.

"Get away!" I shouted, before I even looked.

"Do I have to?" said Mom. "I sort of live here."

She was standing next to a dog. Not just any dog, but a dog with a white belly and a sleek black back.

It was a Bernese mountain dog.

It was Farfel.

She was jumping around as Mom started to pull a giant bag of dog food out of the car. "Give me a hand?" Mom asked me. "This bag is heavy."

But I didn't help. I couldn't move. I just stood there in shock. Farfel jumped on me, up and down, her tail wagging faster than tails had the right to wag. "What's Farfel doing here?"

"Happy birthday," said Mom, still struggling with the dog food bag.

"But I didn't even ask for a dog this year."

Mom shrugged. "Maybe I do know something."

As I said, she was a genius.

I got down on my knees and Farfel began licking my face as if it was covered with bacon. She then wrapped her teeth around her rubber bone. I forgot I was holding it. We played tug-of-war for a moment, but then I let go and threw my arms around her. We could play tug-of-war tomorrow. Or the next day. Or the next. But now, I just wanted to hug her and never let go. I couldn't stop smiling. "Thanks, Mom!" I said. This *was* the best birthday ever, after all.

"You're welcome," she said, bending down and hugging both of us.

I know twelve-year-olds are too old for hugs, but I didn't stop her.

"Does this mean I'm not getting pants for my birthday?" I asked, laughing as Farfel smothered me in licks.

"Maybe just one pair," Mom said, laughing, too. "And sorry again about the basketball game."

"What basketball game?" I asked, hugging Farfel.

Allan Woodrow is the author of *The Pet War* and of the Zachary Ruthless series, as well as other books for young readers, written under secret names. He currently lives near Chicago with his family and two goldfish. The goldfish are vicious. For more about Allan and his books, visit his website at www.allanwoodrow.com.

What is RedRover®?

RedRover is a charity that helps people learn about animals and helps animals when they need us the most.

RedRover sets up shelters for animals who have nowhere to go because of natural disasters, like fires or floods, or have been rescued from lives of pain and suffering, like dogfighting and puppy mills.

RedRover also helps people save their pets' lives by helping to pay for veterinary care when owners don't have the money needed for urgent medical expenses. And RedRover has many ways that animal lovers — like YOU — can take action to stop animal cruelty and neglect.

How do I get involved?

Visit **RedRover.org/Youth** to learn about all the ways you can help animals!

1. Take a **Kindness Pledge** and ask your friends to take the pledge, too.
2. Download a coloring page.
3. Take an animal quiz to test how much you already know about animals.
4. Take the **My Dog Is Cool** pledge and teach others about the dangers of leaving dogs in hot cars.

FOR EDUCATORS AND PARENTS

Founded in 1987, RedRover is a 501(c)3 national nonprofit organization that brings animals out of crisis and strengthens the bond between people and animals through emergency sheltering, disaster relief services, financial assistance, and education.

If you're looking for ways to engage kids and develop empathy and critical thinking skills, the **RedRover Readers** program is a perfect match. The program offers training and lesson plans to help educators teach animal behavior and lead powerful discussions using stories and question strategies that help students:

- Understand perspectives that are different from their own
- Recognize and discuss emotional states
- Analyze information and make humane decisions
- Have more positive social interactions with others
- Think independently from others
- Think creatively
- Feel more empathy

Parents and educators can access free tips, resources, and youth opportunities at **RedRover.org/Readers**.

Learn about our many other animal-related programs at **RedRover.org**.